SIMON RAVEN

THE ISLANDS OF SORROW

and other macabre tales

VALANCOURT BOOKS

The Islands of Sorrow and Other Macabre Tales by Simon Raven
Originally published in two volumes by The Winged Lion as *The Islands of Sorrow* in 1994 and *Remember Your Grammar and Other Haunted Stories* in 1997
First Valancourt Books edition 2025

Published by Valancourt Books, Richmond, Virginia
http://www.valancourtbooks.com

The Valancourt Books name and logo are federally registered trademarks of Valancourt Books, LLC

ISBN 978-1-960241-52-8 (*trade paperback*)
Also available as an ebook.

Cover by Roderick Brydon
Set in Bembo Book MT

THE ISLANDS OF SORROW

SIMON RAVEN was born in London in 1927 and educated at Charterhouse, from which he was expelled in 1945 for homosexual conduct (though it was not his first sexual encounter: he boasted of having been seduced at age nine by the games master, an experience he said gave 'immediate and unalloyed pleasure'). He then performed his national service in the Army until 1948, at which point he enrolled at King's College, Cambridge, to study Classics. After leaving King's College, Raven secured an army commission, serving in Germany and Kenya before being forced to resign (in lieu of court-martial) over his mounting gambling debts. He managed to eke out a living in journalism until he met the young publisher Anthony Blond, who believed in Raven's writing talent and offered to subsidize him while he wrote his first novel, *The Feathers of Death* (1959), on condition that he leave London and its temptations. His relationship with Blond was a fruitful one: the publisher would go onto publish Raven's work over the next three decades, including the spy thriller *Brother Cain* (1959), the classic vampire tale *Doctors Wear Scarlet* (1960), and the ten-volume *Alms for Oblivion* sequence (1964-1976), satirical novels focusing on the English upper class after the Second World War. In later works Raven returned to the interest in horror and the supernatural he had evinced in *Doctors Wear Scarlet*, with the Gothic novels *The Roses of Picardie* (1980) and *September Castle* (1984), the haunting novella *The Islands of Sorrow* (1994), and a collection of short fiction, *Remember Your Grammar and Other Haunted Stories* (1997). After a series of strokes, he died in 2001 at age 73, having written his own epitaph: 'He shared his bottle—and, when still young and appetising, his bed.'

By Simon Raven

Novels and Stories

The Feathers of Death (1959)★
Brother Cain (1959)
Doctors Wear Scarlet (1960)★
Close of Play (1962)
The Fortunes of Fingel (1976)
An Inch of Fortune (1980)
The Roses of Picardie (1980)
September Castle (1984)
The Islands of Sorrow (1994)
Remember Your Grammar and Other Haunted Stories (1997)

The Alms For Oblivion Sequence

The Rich Pay Late (1964)
Friends in Low Places (1965)
The Sabre Squadron (1966)
Fielding Gray (1967)
The Judas Boy (1968)
Places Where They Sing (1970)
Sound the Retreat (1971)
Come Like Shadows (1972)
Bring Forth the Body (1974)
The Survivors (1976)

The First-Born of Egypt Sequence

Morning Star (1984)
The Face of the Waters (1985)
Before the Cock Crow (1986)
New Seed for Old (1988)
Blood of My Bone (1989)
In the Image of God (1990)
The Troubadour (1992)

Other Writings

The English Gentleman (1961)
Boys Will Be Boys (1963)
Royal Foundation and Other Plays (1966)
Shadows on the Grass (1982)
The Old School (1986)
The Old Gang (1988)
Bird of Ill Omen (1989)

★ Also available from Valancourt.

CONTENTS

'Remember Your Grammar' was first published in *The Listener*, 25th December and 1st January 1975; 'The Team Photograph' in *My Lord's*, Willow Books (Harper Collins) 1990; 'The Sarcophagus' in *The Observer*, 5th August 1978; 'The Bottle of 1912' in *The Compleat Imbiber* 4; 'The Amateur' in *Turf Accounts*, Gollancz/Witherby 1994; 'The Proselyte' in *The Printer's Devil*, South East Arts 1991; 'The Caddy' in *One Over Par*, H.F. & G. Witherby 1992; 'The Tric Trac Man' in *Brooks's: A Social History*, Constable and Company 1991; 'Fair Rosamund' in *The Spectator*, 20th December 1980; 'The Guide' in *Punch*, 6th June 1979; and 'The Spirit of Cricket to Come' in *The Field*, June 1987.

THE ISLANDS OF SORROW

'Last night,' said Adam Ogilvie, 'I dreamt I had two pricks.'

'Where was the second one?' I enquired.

'Growing out of the small of my back, just above the crack. I could feel it quite easily with my hand—it appeared to be uncircumcised and without balls—but I couldn't see it. So I massaged it into a very passable erection, and then displayed it to the pier-glass which reflected it back into my shaving mirror, which I arranged at the right angle to give me a good look. And of course it wasn't a penis at all: only a short tail that contained erectile tissue.'

'Oeuf Surprise Connaught, gentlemen,' said Mr Symonds the Head Waiter.

'Montrachet 1947, gentlemen,' said Jamieson the Wine Butler.

When they were gone,

'Did you know that Jamieson was a Regimental Serjeant-Major in the Coldstream?' Adam said. 'He retired three years ago when he found out that the Brigade was still going to accept National Service Officers although the war had been over for seven years. He had no time, he said, for Temporary Gentlemen.'

'He must have put up with a lot worse here. All these Americans.'

'He doesn't mind them. He says that at least they're not masquerading as what they're not. They just have money to spend and spend it.'

'You seem to know a lot about Jamieson.'

'He was with me,' said Adam, 'just after the war. He was a Serjeant then, on detachment to the Military Police, a Special Section of which I commanded. Keeping the streets clean

—to speak metaphorically—in Venice. Any boys and girls
who wanted to sell themselves to the soldiery had to come to
Jamieson and me for a Licence. So did the cat-house keepers, of
course. It was a very lucrative affair for both of us; but we never
got greedy, so nobody complained. Mind you, we had a dozy
doctor—an absolute poppet, but living in a dream-boat—who
missed a nasty dose of clap in one of the girls, who gave it to an
American Brigadier-General. There was nearly a pyrotechnic
complaint *then*, but we fixed up a squad of thirteen-year-olds
for the General, in order to make up. Everything forgiven and a
handsome bonus.'

With wet eyes he looked into the past.

'What reminded me of all this,' he said, 'apart from Jamieson himself, was that dream I had last night. You see, the tail I
dreamt that I saw in my shaving mirror was exactly the same as
the tail on the marble Satyr in the garden of our H.Q.'

'Garden? In Venice?'

'There are just a few. What happened was this. We were
meant to operate—Jamieson and the dozy doctor and I—from
the British Officers' Leave Hotel, the Luna, which is, and was,
bang in the centre of Venice. Jamieson got fed up with "the
Temporary Gentlemen" who came there, and I got fed up with
officious majors, who seemed to think I was responsible for
running the hotel and not just the whores, so I fixed up with
a Venetian Carabiniere with whom I liaised from time to time
to take a large flat in a run-down Palazzo which he knew of . . .
between the Church of St-Alvise and the Madonna del Orto.'

'A tidy distance from the centre,' I said.

'Yes. But the fancy girls and boys could find it easily enough
when they wanted their licences renewed, whereas no bloody
Staff Officer even knew where it was.'

'How did the American Brigadier-General get in touch
about his clap?'

'He happened before we moved to the Palazzo Baldinucci
. . . which was where we were installed in a third floor flat, by
my chum the Comandante Piero Corvino. The Venetian Cara-

binieri had some sort of control over the place; I found out why
a little later. I also found out that we, as foreigners, should never
have been allowed within a mile of it, and certainly would not
have been, had not Corvino needed our money and our help
to keep his new mistress in goodies from the black market. But
when all that was said, it was a very pleasant establishment. The
rooms were tall, the furniture was stylish if rickety, the food,
which came in from a nearby cook-shop, was imaginative. Our
flat, where we slept as well as worked, looked out, in front, on a
Canal with a few more crumbly palaces the other side of it, and,
at the rear, on our garden. This was a bosky affair with pine and
sweet shrubs and lady birch. It stretched from a terrace under
our back wall to the shore of the Laguna Morta. There was a
small muddy beach—no quay or proper landing place—some
tiny dunes with long, spiky grass to mark the border between
the beach and the garden, and just in from the dunes a little dell
or grotto, at the bottom of which the marble Satyr pranced
about with a corkscrew erection in front and a tail like mine in
my dream sticking out at the top of his crack. He was just four
foot high, and in the early summer the wild flowers twisted
round his shaggy legs and right up to his hooky nose and the
budding horns on his forehead. There was a semi-circular stone
bench on the rim of the hollow; and sitting there, in the shade
of an ilex, we could look down into the glen where the Satyr
piped and danced, and so to the miniature dunes and the mud
beach and the Laguna Morta, and across the still waters to San
Michele, the Island of the Dead. Most of the day we sat there,
Jamieson and the Doctor and I; when the lads and lassies came
to be licensed and examined, the Doctor had them strip naked
down in the dell by the Satyr, on whose corkscrew cock some
of the girls (and boys) would do little tricks to ingratiate themselves—'

'—No wonder the doctor missed that case of clap—'

'—And the whole thing,' said Adam, 'was a magic idyll in
that summer after the war ... until one day a small barge ran
up on to our beach and began to unload a group of passengers,

ten of them, five men and five women, all dressed in long white overalls, almost down to their ankles, like the coats worn by umpires at county matches before the war, at Old Trafford or Trent Bridge or Canterbury,' Adam said, lingering with love on the last, then, coming back from a dream of Canterbury to his tale of Venice: 'ten white walkers, who came over the little dunes, skirted the dell and our bench without apparently seeing us, and wandered through the garden towards the terrace and the Palazzo like the mild-eyed, melancholy lotus eaters in Tennyson's poem. Of all this Jamieson and my dream have reminded me—and of a very great deal more.'

'Drink,' I said, filling his glass with Montrachet: 'drink and tell.'

On the evening of the afternoon on which the visitors had descended on the garden of the Palazzo Baldinucci (Adam Ogilvie told me over the Montrachet) Adam went to see the Comandante Piero Corvino, who liked to drink at Florian's, wearing rather seedy plain clothes, between the hours of seven and eight. The Comandante favoured the interior of the Café, as the pigeons of the Piazza annoyed him; and inside Adam found him, in the chamber which displays on one wall the portrait of a lady who looks like a fading courtesan trying to drum up trade by impersonating the Madonna, thus creating an appetising prospect for a clientele of male and female penitents. The room had the air of *temps jadis* that Florian's is said to have possessed from the day it first opened in the 18th Century; always shabby (if distinguished), its appearance had not suffered in the least from the total lack of repair or refurbishment during the five years since 1940.

'*Buona sera, Signore*,' said the Comandante to Adam. 'Refreshment?'

'Red vermouth. Thank you.'

The Comandante rang his glass with a spoon and ordered from a waiter who crept up like a crab.

'No trouble at the Baldinucci . . . I 'ope?' the Comandante said.

'No trouble. Just some slightly peculiar arrivals.'

Adam described the disembarkation of the lotus-eaters.

'They are the tenants of the second floor. You did not think you would be 'aving the 'ole Palazzo?'

'All ten of them? On one floor?'

'The Palazzo is spacious. They will not be there long. They will not disturb you.'

'*Il Comandante* will excuse me . . . but their mere demeanour is disturbing.'

'But very peaceful. Or did not *Il Capitano* find it so?'

'Too peaceful. They were like sleep-walkers. It was as if they had been heavily drugged.'

'Oh come, Adam,' said Corvino, who liked to switch rapidly from the formal to the familiar, and then back just as quickly. 'We admire you *Inglesi*—at least the gentlemen among you— because you 'ave such capacity for minding your own business, for never making fuss. 'Ere is clearly no business of yours and nothing for fussing. Five men and five women, all very tired from their duties, arriving for a well needed period of rest.'

'So you know the exact composition of the party?'

'I know all about the party. Almost everything there is to be known. But I tell you it is no concern of yours. And you, with your beautiful Inglesi manners, with your courtesy of an Officer and a gentleman, will surely accept that. And so will the good Serjeant Jamieson, if only because you will tell 'im to, and so will the *egregio dottore*, if only so that he can go on fiddling so fondly *le ragazze*.'

'Oh yes, Piero,' said Adam. 'We are all very happy in the Palazzo. The last thing we want is to make trouble.'

'Then why, *Signore Capitano*, all this *fastidio* about the "demeanour" of the new arrivals? 'Ere I am, during my quiet of the day, and you come in and start wailing like a *mendicante*.'

'I did not wail, *Signore Comandante*, I merely enquired.'

'And now your enquiry is answered.'

'It would be, Piero,' said Adam, 'but for one thing. One of the party dropped this on the way through the garden.'

Adam and the Comandante were alone in the Chamber of the Putana-Madonna. Although the Venetians liked Corvino, they tended (knowing who he was despite his dress) to steer clear of him. Adam was thus at liberty to show his exhibit. He produced a handkerchief from the left breast-pocket of his Service Dress tunic, unwrapped a small, sealed glass phial, and showed the Comandante what appeared to be a human eye-ball pickled in some translucent yellow liquid. Above the Iris and slightly to its left, as they looked at it, was a small lesion of malignant mauve.

'Very well,' said Piero Corvino, ringing his glass for the crabby waiter; 'I shall 'ave to explain a little further.'

The diseased eye (the Comandante told Adam in Florian's) was a specimen being brought into Venice for examination in a laboratory. He would now take it and see that it went where it ought. It should not have been entrusted to anyone in the party, a leave party it was, for all of them were in a state of exhaustion and semi-sedation, unfit to undertake any errand of delicacy. Clearly, discipline was growing slack on the island from which they had come. The end of the war had induced a damaging euphoria in a number of places and institutions. Not that the work done by the members of the leave party on their island had anything to do with war—very far from it—but there was a lot of *far niente* in the air these days.

Thus and thus. As the Captain Ogilvie must be well aware, the Lagoon was full of islands ... islands of religion, asylum, quarantine, incarceration, islands of learning like San Lazzaro (where the good monks had taught Armenian to the *Inglese* Milor Byron), islands of mental aberration like San Servolo, islands of naval and military storage and preparation, islands of murderous lunacy, islands of dead men's bones (fetched out of their original graves to make room for others), islands of the most bizarre disease. Some of these islands, like San Francesco del Deserto, were relatively large and well known: others, further away, were tiny and obscure, presenting a makeshift landing stage and a few shacks, possibly a Shooting Lodge, occasionally the elegant Villa of an eccentric or misanthrope, more often the bare stone buildings necessary to house the hopelessly sick or deformed who, with those that cared for them and possibly an outcast fisher or two, made up the only residents.

It was from one such that the leave party which had arrived at the Baldinucci had come that afternoon. Their labours were so horrible that they were granted periods of recuperation equal to their periods of actual employment—a month on and then a month off. Those on furlough in the Baldinucci would now have two weeks of rest, accompanied by medical and mental examination and treatment, and followed by two weeks of holiday in any area, within Italian territory, of their choice. All the Comandante was prepared to say was that they amply deserved this indulgence. He was aware that Captain Ogilvie, an English Officer from the finest Regiment of all (though at present attached to the Military Police for Special Service) would respect this confidence, would in no way trouble the already troubled souls with whom he now shared the Palazzo, and, should he chance to encounter any of them, would treat them with the gentleness and geniality for which the *Inglesi* (he raised his glass of Raki to Adam) were so well and justly loved throughout all *Italia*. . . .

'A bit of an exaggeration, that last bit,' said Adam to Serjeant Jamieson in the Flat occupied by The Pox Poopers (a sobriquet of the Doctor's invention) later that evening. 'But the message was very plain, Serjeant. "You know what I've told you, and that's all you're ever going to know, and if you try to find out any more you'll be abusing your privilege and our trust." '

'And that eye, sir?'

'Obviously from a patient on the island they came from.'

'And it just fell out of its socket? Or was removed during an operation? And what was the matter with it?'

'Just the sort of question we are forbidden to ask and in any case will go unanswered. Where's the doctor?'

'Pissed in Aldo's Bar, sir. The one by the second bridge down.'

'Go and fetch him out, would you mind? Too much "genial-ity", as Corvino might say, is not a good thing. The natives will take advantage. Just tell him I want a word with him.'

'No trouble, sir. The doctor is docility itself.'

However (as Adam told me over the Montrachet) more than docility was required of Lieutenant Fotheringay R.A.M.C. by the time the Serjeant got him back. On the stairs, which led past the quarters of the party on furlough and up to the Pox Poop-ers' flat, was sprawled a handsome if rather elongated girl, with red hair and an ashen face, dressed in the white overalls worn by every member of the party when they had landed on the beach that afternoon. She appeared to have paid no attention to her dress or her person since her arrival. Not that Fotheringay or Serjeant Jamieson took in such details at first; the stair was so dark that they tripped over her. The Serjeant recovered at once while Fotheringay went arse over tit, and both bellowed up to Adam to come and help. Order was restored, the girl, after quick consultation ('Might have something interesting to say, sir, when she comes round'), was carried up and spread on a *chaise longue* which was barely long enough. Fotheringay, not too drunk to know a good thing when he saw one, carried out a detailed and intimate examination of the girl, while Jamieson and Adam, as was their wont during the inspection of would-be *demi-mondaines*, rather avidly watched.

'Exhaustion plus dope,' Fotheringay said, patting the girl's red pubic patch: 'possibly laudanum. Same effect anyway.'

At this stage the girl came to, lowered her dress over her *privata* (she wore no underclothes) without comment or com-plaint, and enquired in a quiet voice and correct English (with a slight and repetitious lilt) where she was and who were assem-bled about her. She was civilly answered by Adam, who con-fined himself to saying that they were a British Security Section which was stationed within the Palazzo. This she understood without difficulty; and when asked what she was doing on the stairway, deposed that she had been for a stroll on the terrace and had been confused while returning because 'last time we were in a higher apartment'.

Did she now feel able to return to her proper quarters?

Yes; but could she stay a little longer? She would not be missed—her companions were all asleep and in any case would not worry about her until the morning.

'Are you sure of that?' said Adam. 'My information is that for the first part of your ... your holiday ... you are all kept together.'

'And from whom did you have this information?'

Adam told her.

'It is no concern of his. He is under orders to make certain that accommodation is available for us and for those who replace us when it is their time to come to Venice. Two or three Palazzi are used for this purpose, so that different parties of workers do not meet even in passing.' She began to babble a bit. 'There is no reason to keep the parties apart, in fact every reason not to, as we might compare experience. But during this war everyone is suspicious about everything and nothing, and they hate people to talk to anybody about anything. The system of the war-time remains. Men like Corvino are pleased by that —it makes things easier for them if all of us in the party stay together and do not stray. But we, the ten of us, are friends and do not spy on ourselves.'

'Is no one in charge?'

'We are all equal. Medical attendants. Thus, there is no master or mistress of us, but there is one called "Caporale" who keeps the lists and so on, and will make sure we are all attended to by the doctors and other officials who begin to come tomorrow. This Caporale—he is our friend too. He will not mind where I am until the morning, when the doctors come. Let me stay the night here. I wish to be away from them.'

'Away from your friends?'

'I have been with them a long time. Where we come from the length of time is doubled, trebled, even one hundredfold.

I must have change. Just for this one night. There can be no harm.'

'She has said that twice too often,' Jamieson said to Adam.

If she heard this remark she ignored it. She now made it evident, by the simple and shameless expedient of taking both his hands and pulling him down towards her, that the 'change' she needed would take the form of Lieutenant Fotheringay.

'I love a bit of ginge,' he said.

'My name is Formosa,' she said.

'Very apt,' said Jamieson gallantly.

'Food first,' said Fotheringay. 'Bread, soup and a little wine.'

'You have had enough wine, I think. What is your name?'

'Richard,' said Fotheringay. 'Don't worry. I come out of it very quickly.'

He loped off on his gangling legs to the kitchen, his round silly face blazing like a full moon.

'No need for you lot to hang about,' he called back to Adam and Serjeant Jamieson.

The empty Montrachet bottle was taken away and replaced by Léoville-Las-Cases. Mr Symonds served the Woodcock.

Jamieson said to Adam, as he poured the wine:

'Talking about the old days in Venice, sir?'

'Yes, Serjeant-Major. Do you mind?'

'Not in the least, sir. It was great fun at the beginning, wasn't it? In the garden, with the Satyr and all those boys and girls. Only when that lot came from the island—'

Jamieson looked at me and shook his head.

'Ah well,' he said, 'I'll let you find out for yourself. Captain Ogilvie is not the kind to miss much out.'

'I don't want him to miss anything out.'

Jamieson shook his head again. He and Symonds retired.

'Well?' I said to Adam.

'The morning after Formosa came to us, she left very early,' he said. 'Later on Fotheringay and I walked in the garden....'

Fotheringay had been very eager to talk (Adam told me over the Woodcock).

'She started coming almost at once,' Fotheringay had said: 'she kept on interminably. Quivering and throbbing and jerking and writhing—all six foot three of her. I thought she'd go to sleep afterwards, but instead, without any prompting, she started to talk, very slowly and clearly, as if I were a child to be instructed in a difficult subject. . . .'

'The island—it is little more than a bank of mud—is called Marciume,' Formosa had said to Richard Fotheringay: 'you know what Marciume means in your language? It means "decay". Everything about the island is decaying. The earth is poisoned, there are no flowers, no shrubs or even sea-grass. Every building, every article of furniture is infected with maggots or fungus.

'But the most decayed of all are the people, the people whom my friends and I try to serve. They have an illness for which there is no name; an illness which disfigures them so that they must wear masks, like the old Venetian domino. And we who care for them must wear special costumes which isolate our whole bodies: special helmets with cylinders of oxygen like divers, special coverings over our overalls, special boots like a fisherman's from foot to fork. We communicate with our patients only by signs, as they communicate with each other. Some say they had a language once; but this is long gone; most of them have no lips, no teeth, to enunciate. There is little we can do for them . . . except show that we are fellow human beings who wish to ease their suffering. We provide such food as they can eat, such bedding as their rotting bodies can rest on; we maintain such cleanliness as is possible. For the rest, we live together in an isolated cabin. We pass into this through a special chamber of disinfection, in which we take off our helmets and garments of protection. Once inside our refuge, we eat food from tins and sleep in a dormitory—there is no room for anything else. We read, we play chess and cards and backgammon;

and we make love, as we must, in public . . . a mere evacuation, at best, a brief escape from an eternity of despair. Do you wonder that I wish to be parted from my friends—and they *are* my friends—for this one night?'

'All of which was all very well—or all very ill,' said Adam Ogilvie to me after the Woodcock and over the Crêpes; 'but it had been told to Richard in general terms and raised many particular and so far unanswered questions. What was the cause of this illness, its origins, its essence: what was its ending? Where did the patients come from? To what extent were Formosa and her colleagues jailers as well as nurses? What, more precisely, were the symptoms? How long did the sufferers survive, and where were they buried?

'No business of ours, you might say. But by now we were very curious. As a doctor, Richard Fotheringay, however slapdash in practice, was fascinated by medical history and theory. He was by no means as vacuous as he looked: he simply found that the simulation of personal pottiness was a great aid to personal independence. Serjeant Jamieson too was interested: clearly the island and its inhabitants posed a hideous problem of administration and logistics, and Jamieson much enjoyed considering such problems and methods, both current and putative, for their solution. In short, we all needed something to engage our energy and intelligence, for by now the organisation of venal Venetian venery was merely a matter of routine, and we were delighted that chance had thrown us this succulent item to investigate.'

For the next few days (Adam told me) there was much coming and going, on the Canal, of official boats bearing men in a variety of Police uniforms or very sharply cut dark suits. The boats would turn into the Canal from the Sacco della Misericordia, proceed a short way past the Madonna del Orto, then turn right under a small bridge and down a narrow Rio, on the left of which were steps leading up from the water to a beautiful doorway with an Ogival arch. This was the way by which all official visitors to the furlough party in the Palazzo Baldinucci arrived and departed. They came and left at all hours. Neither Adam nor the other two under his command saw anything more of Formosa or any of her friends, except between the hours of noon and two p.m., during which they strolled or sat on the terrace, making it plain by their demeanour that they neither desired nor expected to be accosted by any of them.

One day, however, when Fotheringay was hanging about on the little bridge over the entrance to the Rio and enjoying the view up and down the Canal, he spotted an acquaintance who was departing in a motor boat flying an imposing military flag. Fotheringay shouted down, his acquaintance shouted up, and the next afternoon Fotheringay brought him to the bench over the Satyr's dell. He was wearing the uniform of the Italian Army Medical Department and was introduced by Fotheringay as the Colonnello Francesco Cinquemani.

'He will be out of the Army in a few days,' Fotheringay explained: 'he is a lecturer in forensic and social medicine at Padua. Like myself he prefers theory to practice. He has been questioning . . . our new neighbours . . . about their patients.'

Apparently Fotheringay had met him, a few days before, in the Medical Library attached to the Hospital in the Campo Zanipolo. They had both been looking for the same volume —on the relation of the Great Plague of Athens during the 5th Century B.C. to the Black Death—and both located it at the same moment. Fotheringay had deferred to Cinquemani's rank, while Cinquemani had yielded to Fotheringay as his country's 'saviour and guest', whereupon they had both burst into tears and kissed each other, then together examined in detail the opulent ceiling, the Library having once been the Chapter Room of the great Scuola di San Marco. They had agreed to dine some days later: chance had hastened reunion.

Fotheringay now repeated, for the Colonnello's benefit, all that Formosa had told him, which of course the Colonnello knew already with a great deal more. When Adam hinted that a few more details would be appreciated, Francesco Cinquemani shook his head and said that he was only a student of the whole affair: he was privileged to make his enquiries as a man of science and under strict pledge of secrecy. However,

'Some things I think I may tell you,' he said, 'as my good friend here is also a historian of medicine—'

'—Would-be historian,' said modest Richard.

'—And the bond between scholars is more important than pedantic observance of official requirements. Thus I can tell you that what these unhappy islanders are suffering from is an aggravated form of leprosy brought back to Venezia from a place to the East. The sufferers were spotted by medical experts and placed in quarantine. There was only the one group. None other has since appeared with such an illness. The matter is thus securely contained.'

Cinquemani giggled slightly as though aware that he had revealed nothing. He shook his head again, then nodded it, as though conceding that he would now try to do better for his hosts.

'Like any form of leprosy,' he said, 'even the most virulent, it is not nearly as contagious as you might imagine. The elaborate precautions which the nurses take to prevent contact with their patients are due more to distaste on their part than to actual danger; a device to assist their morale. Or again, the masks worn by the diseased are to conceal unsightliness rather than assist in cure.'

Cinquemani giggled again.

'I have still told you little enough,' he said.

'Are you implying,' said Adam, 'that it is not necessary for the nurses to live, as they live, in complete anti-sepsis and isolation?'

'That . . . is very necessary,' the Colonnello said.

'But if the precautions they take while they work are too elaborate, where is the need for such absolute segregation when they are at leisure?'

The Colonel shrugged and smiled.

'The nurses do not wish . . . amorous advances . . . from disfigured patients who seek something wholesome. Officials do not wish heavy claims against the public purse on this ground or other.'

'Then the patients retain sexual capacity?'

'It is wise to assume so.'

There was a thoughtful pause.

'How long will it be,' said Jamieson, 'before they all die and you can close this quarantine station?'

The Colonel gave Jamieson a sharper look than such a humdrum question merited.

'They will die in God's good time,' he averred.

'This illness will not hasten their death?'

'Not noticeably . . . so far.'

'Did it ever seem desirable,' Jamieson pursued, 'what with the war and the problems of administration and man power, of valuable resources diverted to Marciume which were so badly needed elsewhere—did it ever seem desirable to impose, let us say, a final solution?'

'Of course,' said Cinquemani, poker-faced; 'or so I hear. You must understand that I had no part in this, I am simply allowed to make enquiries *at this time* in the pursuit of knowledge. But as I understand what I have heard, it seemed very desirable to make a final solution. The matter was much discussed. In the end, however, such a proceeding was deemed inadvisable.'

'For moral reasons?'

'For what other?' said the Colonel shiftily.

Another thoughtful pause.

'Research, perhaps,' said Richard Fotheringay. 'The disease is rare if not unique. Apparently this variant of leprosy has only been found in this one group of people, all of whom, I presume, picked it up in the same region?'

'I think so.'

'What region?'

'The island of Naxos.'

'Naxos? In the Aegean. *Not* very far East. And a perfectly healthy place.'

'Not so healthy, perhaps, during hard times.'

'I see,' said Jamieson: 'during war? War, starvation, destitution, destruction, pestilence.'

'That would be so,' said the Colonel. 'Oh yes: that would certainly be so.'

'Then they contracted the illness during wartime in Naxos. And brought it back from there. During the war?'

The Colonnello hesitated.

'During time of war,' he said: 'siege and wrack.'

'We must remember our duties as hosts,' said Adam, seeing a wan look on Cinquemani's face. 'Whisky, Colonel Cinquemani? Serjeant Jamieson brought some down in case.'

'Wine, since I see it there. My friends,' said Francesco Cinquemani as Adam filled a glass with a brisk red wine from the Veneto, 'I can tell you no more. Not directly.'

'Not for the fellowship of scholars?' Richard Fotheringay said.

'I can tell you no more, for I am on oath; but I can show you something, and even explain it, up to a point. After that point you must make your own deductions about . . . about the underlying reality.'

'One of the nurses brought a pickled eye from the island.'

'Doubtless for experiment. It is no eye, nor other part of the anatomy, that I have to show you. It is a place.'

'Naxos?'

'Not Naxos. Somewhere here in Venezia.'

'Where? What? How far?'

'You will see when we get there.'

'Colonel Cinquemani,' Adam continued over the Port, 'led the three of us over a bridge across our Canal and along a passage-way decorated with low-relief carvings of Saracens and Camels, and so to a Canal parallel with our own. Here we turned right and proceeded towards the Campo Ghetto-Nuova. The Palaces grew shabbier and taller, the Rios which led off the Canal narrower and dirtier. Washing lines stretched over the

Rios, from window to opposite window, hung with curious garments. We crossed an iron bridge (over the main Canal) into a tiny Campo, then went over a steep, sharply arched bridge with no balustrades ("Good job we're sober") into a tunnel, turned right down another tunnel so narrow that we must proceed in Indian file, and came into a Courtyard which was about ten yards square. A curiously written but decipherable sign to our left announced this as the Campo Lamorea; a Romanesque Archway to our right led us into an even smaller yard, designated the Campo di Naxos; and a square opening perhaps four foot high (labelled Sotto-Passaggio degli Sognatori) ran through forty yards of pitch darkness to a dank, slimy Campo, about thirty yards square, bounded by walls so high one had thought one was at the bottom of a deep well. There was no aperture in any of the walls at lower than twenty feet; but an elegant and balustraded stairway, at the far end from where we had emerged stooping and gasping, led up to a very early Gothic doorway (arch above it scarcely pointed).

' "The Campo degli Sognatori",' Colonel Cinquemani said: ' "the Field of Dreamers." '

Adam and I were now alone in the Grill Room. Jamieson approached us, not, as I had supposed, to ask us to move into the lounge or the bar, but to enquire what point Adam had reached in his story.

'You'd hardly credit it,' Jamieson said; 'each of those little squares was a district in its own right, with its own customs, cuisine and dialect—and about sixty inhabitants. Some of them had never even been as far as the next Campo; only about half of them outside the confines of the Ghetto, and not one of them out of Venice. They were, to say the least, inbred. Jewish? Only in part. The point was, you see, that the Jews and the Ghetto had only been in that area since the 16th Century, when they were moved there from the Giudecca. Before the Jews came, there had been an iron foundry (Campo della Ferriera) operated by the aboriginals, so to speak, the people that had come from

Torcello, before anyone else at all, to escape the plague and the fever.

'I went into it all, gentlemen, later on ... though what the Colonnello told us at the time was plain enough. A large detachment of men from the foundry in the Campo della Ferriera, sick of the heavy labour and the low pay in the ironworks, accompanied what we should call the 4th Crusade to Greece at the beginning of the 13th Century. At first they assisted in the conquest of the Morea, or Peloponnese, and then, when mercenary soldiers were less in demand, they used their skills as ironworkers and heavy carpenters to help build the castles which feudal lords were setting up all over Greece. They were particularly useful in manufacturing the frameworks for catapults and siege mechanisms. Then they were tempted by a munificent offer from Mario Sanudi, who founded the Venetian Duchy of Naxos, to which they repaired in about 1208. They assisted the Duke in the building and arming of ramparts and citadel, but left him, with his reluctant permission, when he transferred his allegiance from the Doge to the Latin Emperor. They then returned to Venice, rather rich by their standards, rebuilt the Campo della Ferriera as the Campo Lamorea, named of course after the Morea, and added the Campo di Naxos.'

'And the Campo degli Sognatori?' I said. 'The Field of the Dreamers?'

'Ah. Captain Ogilvie will tell you about that, sir. So I'll leave him to get on with his story.' And to Adam, 'I've another decanter of Port for you both, sir, and when I've brought it to you, I'll be off. So will Mister Symonds. Stay as late as you like. The Night Porter will cope when you've gone.'

Now there was light at our table only. The slight glow beyond the entrance to the Grill lit only the Head Waiter's high desk, at which Mr Symonds could stand as he wrote.

'The Campo degli Sognatori?' I said to Adam. 'Is that what Cinquemani wanted to show you?'

'He wanted to show us what was behind the Gothic door at

the top of the stairway,' Adam said. 'But before I tell you about that, you must know more of what happened to our gang of ironworkers when they came home from Naxos. As Jamieson said, he went into all this in the City Archives. In those days quite a lot of these were still in Sansovino's Library, where I used to join him from time to time. A pleasure to work there; the wartime closure still kept the public out. Well, one day Jamieson and I came across a correspondence between one of the Doge's secretaries and the Commissioner for Licensing and Ranking the Serenissima's Courtesans. Rather fascinating, as it was pretty well the same job we were doing seven hundred years later.'

The sum of the correspondence (Adam told me in the dark of the Grill) was as follows:—

Epistola de Alessandro Osmarino (Nobili Homine)
  Altissimo Comite Officii Dogalis
  Rei Publicae Serenissimae Venezianae
  ad Federicum Barlinum (Nobilem Hominem)
  Magistrum Officii Stuprorum
  id. mai. a.d. mcxi

Ad Maiorem Dei Gloriam
Egregi Magister,
Salve.
Nuntii quidam certiores nos fecerunt . . . Certain agents of ours have informed us that in the region of the Iron Foundry in the *parrochia* of the Misericordia there has arisen a new type of insidious disease, both among men and among women, which may be due to the unchecked operation of public prostitutes. The disease produces a rash of mauve-coloured ulcers which devour the skin and the flesh, at first almost painlessly, but later, as the ulcers near the bone and reveal nerves and sinews, bringing hideous agony to sufferers.

Quaere et dic celerrime. . . . Investigate and report with all speed.

And from the worthy *Magister Stuprorum* about a month later:

. . . scio non coepisse de mentulis et feminum pudendis, ut mala syphilitica et similia. . . . I am satisfied that this [illness] does not start in the penis, or in the female parts, as does the disease of syphilis and those associated. According to the learned leech, Messer Jacobo Messalino, this new illness was recently brought back by a party of itinerant artisans from the Island and Duchy of Naxos. He opines that it is an hitherto unknown and more than usually malignant strain of leprosy.

From the rather scant evidence, Messer Messalino deduces that the disease was contracted from the contaminated waters of a Well in the Naxian Acropolis, which tradition maintains has its supply from a Spring where the Lady Ariadne had dalliance with the Divine Bacchus. The Spring was choked and diverted during the erection of an earlier fort, thus insulting Bacchus and his mistress (later his bride). The waters of the Well and those that drink them were therefore plagued thenceforth with the Curse of the God. The Well is intermittently sullied by some deposit which, being consumed with the liquid, eats away human flesh.

However this may be, all those who sailed back diseased from Naxos, and those, mercifully few, infected by them since, are now confined in a spacious and well conducted Ospedale which occupies all four sides of a new built Square or Campo, which is separated from the nearest habitation (the Campo di Naxos) by a long, low tunnel. The devoted Messer Messalino and his fellow apothecaries are attending the sick and seeking a cure, so far without success. They have, nevertheless, distilled a chemical which calms and coddles the diseased, to the extent that they apprehend not the true horror of their condition. Comforted by the cordial, they move in the manner of sleep-walkers, even and untroubled, intent on peripety and not on evil-doing, so that they are known as the *sognatori*, the dreamers, and both Hospital and Campo are now named accordingly.

And from the Doge's Palace to Messer Jacobo Messalino:

... certiores nos fac de doloribus mortis istorum et de moribus sepulturae ... inform us about the death agonies of these wretches and the manner of their burial ...

And from Messer Messalino to the Dogal Office:

My patients are mostly young and of strong constitution. Despite the speed with which the pest mounts to its fiercest esculation of the flesh, only two have actually died, and these through accidentally being given excessive measure of the syrup with which I medicine them rather than of the plague itself. The two cadavers were shipped swiftly out of the city and buried in a small deserted island N.E. of Torcello.

To revert to the living, it would appear that when the disease has ravaged the carnal and muscular envelopes to the last degree it then becomes quiescent, leaving the patient totally lethargic, without pain if also without pulp. I must also report that my patients remain capable of desire and propagation, even in the extreme stages of degeneration, and despite the opiate effects of my nostrum and the stupor which, as reported in my previous sentence, descends upon them after their flesh has been devoured. Three live infants have so far been dropped from three separate wombs in this my Hospice: in all cases the babes appeared sound in body for the first twenty days, but then, though continuing to grow normally, developed symptoms of the pest.

May I recommend myself and my poor endeavours, and also the loyal and laborious comrades of my trials, to the mighty and merciful members of the Council ...

'All these details,' said Adam after reciting this summary of official letters, 'were gathered by Jamieson and myself some little time later, when the whole business was further advanced.'

'How did Serjeant Jamieson know enough Latin to work on these documents?'

'Self taught. He took a correspondence course in Latin while in hospital after being wounded in the Desert. Intellectually a very active and accurate man, Jamieson, and usually correct in his conclusions. Now as he, Jamieson, told you, what Cinquemani had said, before he knocked on the Gothic door and took us through it, gave us pretty well the gist of the whole thing—if we'd been sharp enough to grasp it. But we weren't. We just couldn't see where the real enormity lay.'

'You mean there's worse to come?' I said.

'Oh yes,' said Adam. 'Now, you're getting the luxury guest treatment. You're being told—now—much of what we didn't learn nearly so early in the plot. Can you see what's coming?'

'A great deal of human misery,' I said. 'A great deal of self-sacrifice to alleviate it.... At some stage, I suppose, the transfer of the unhappy inmates of the Ospedale degli Sognatori to the Island of Marciume...'

'Nothing else—even with the hints you've had?'

'Nothing else.'

'Very well,' said Adam. 'On to the next stage. As I say, Cinquemani had given us an adequate *histoire* during our walk and while we were recovering from the effects of getting through that tunnel. Having well primed us, then, he now led us up the stairway, knocked on the Gothic door—whereupon it was opened unto him by a character dressed up in surgical kit, turbaned but not masked and with a nice pink face. His two upper front teeth were slightly crossed and he was called Doctor Thrasymedes, being distantly of Greek descent. After a few civil words with Francesco Cinquemani, he showed us round the old Ospedale degli Sognatori, with a commentary as he went....'

'This used to be the chapel,' Thrasymedes had said, leading them through a skeletal chancel to a door on the left of where the altar had been, 'and this is where I do my chemical research. Mind the step as you enter. All modern equipment, as you see, no instruments or substances denied us even during the war, with plenty of room for myself and my two assistants, who are presently resting.' He pointed down the long laboratory to a door at the far end. 'We all live in quarters which are situated over the tunnel—but these will be of no interest to you. What may amuse you is our Museum, to reach which we must go back the way we have come, through the chapel and the entrance vestibule, to the opposite side of the building.

'So. Our Museo degl' Ammalati. On your left you see the *cadavere*, preserved in chemicals, of a patient from Marciume who died five years ago. You will notice that the pest has operated in furrows rather than in blotches or single sores. You will also notice that the patient, having been attacked long before death by the last stages of the disease, has developed a kind of film which covers and protects, though it does not conceal, the entire surface of the afflicted body. Having passed through the most horrible period of visible decay, the body has, in a manner, healed itself; and we know that at this stage a kind of numbness comes over the sufferer, a condition of torpor. This does not lead directly to death; the patient may survive for many years in this stage. In the case of the cadaver on exhibition, death was due to an ordinary cardiac arrest.

'Perhaps I should make it plain to you, before we go any further, that although a passable *modus vivendi* has been evolved for our patients, we are no nearer an absolute cure of the disease than our predecessors of seven hundred years ago.

'Here is an eyeball which was brought in the other day. Notice the mauve lesion above the iris; this is a rare instance in which the disease has attacked the eye and threatened the frontal lobes of the brain, thus necessitating the eye's prompt removal in an elementary operation which can be carried out by nurses on Marciume itself.

'Here on my right is a baby which died still-born: perfect, you see, in every respect ... as compared with this little body, that of an infant who died thirty days after birth, and already bears the earlier ravages—notice the strip of infected tissue from chin to navel. Another example, this time of a female patient who died at the age of well over eighty; you will observe that she too developed the film which clothes the body in a protective envelope and somehow brings it to a semblance of comfort.

'And finally, the bones of a young man who killed himself in about 1450, some five hundred years ago, just before the inhabitants of this Hospital were transferred to Marcium. He committed suicide while suffering from the climax of the pest's attack on his nervous system. I should explain that if, as in this case, a patient dies before the formation of the protective film, his body rots in the normal manner. If, however, he dies after the covering has formed, the covering will preserve the corpse for a considerable time ... though for permanent preservation we must use tanks of chemicals, as in the earlier examples I showed you.

'And that is almost all, I think. In case you are wondering what the rooms in the fourth side of the Campo contain, you should know that there are kept the records of hundreds of years of research and experiment. The rooms resemble the Sibyl's Cave in proliferation and disorder of documents, most of them in any case rendered indecipherable by half a millennium of neglect and damp. Why has no effort been made to keep them well arranged and in good condition? Because earlier Masters of the Ospedale were not always very attentive to research, regarding the prospects as hopeless; while later Masters often drew the salaries for Assistants and Curators theoretically responsible for the documents without actually employing the personnel. However, the results of all research carried out since 1700 have been efficiently filed and stored in a section of the City Archives, and have remained there unharmed and readily available to proper and authorised persons.

'Finally, why are the worthless parchments and papers in the storage rooms not removed and destroyed? Because of the disagreeable labour involved in getting them out of this Campo through the long, low tunnel by which you gentlemen approached and which is, in fact, the only means of approach, now as when the Ospedale was first founded.'

At the conclusion of the tour (Adam continued in the umbrageous Grill Room) the Colonnello, Fotheringay, Jamieson and

Adam himself repaired to the Station Buffet, not far away, for refreshment. Dottore Thrasymedes was invited to come too, but declined.

'If you think the Station an odd choice,' said Francesco Cinquemani, 'remember that the Ferrovie dello Stato are indeed "of the State", and their Restaurants are better provided than all but the most luxurious and costly of private establishments.'

To support his assertion they were now served a very decent collation of hot and cold sea-snacks and delicatessen, with a robust white wine from the Veneto.

'And now,' said the Colonnello, 'I have told you all that I can without breaking my official pledges. Possibly more than I should. Captain Ogilvie, kindly summarise your conclusions as a layman.'

'The disease came from Naxos,' said Adam, 'probably a special form of leprosy contracted in the special conditions there in about 1208, though the cause is unspecified save by reference to an amusing but unhelpful myth about Bacchus and Ariadne. Sufferers were at first thought to have some kind of venereal disorder, e.g. the form of syphilis which was common in Eastern Europe centuries before Columbus imported the really murderous strain hatched in America; but the venereal theory was soon refuted through observation of the symptoms. From the beginning these could be modified, up to a point, but not cured. In about 1450 the sufferers, presumably because of their numbers, were taken from the Ospedale degli Sognatori to the Island of Marciume. Sexual intercourse between patients was practised and subsequent procreation was possible, though the former was discouraged by the drug administered to them and, one imagines, severally curtailed in older patients by the physical encapsulation and mental placidity which overcame them after the ferocious climax of this pest—or whatever you care to call it.'

'All right,' said Cinquemani; 'now you, Richard Fotheringay, as a medical man. . . .'

'I have little to add to what Adam has said. It would seem, from what I heard from the nurse, Formosa, that at one stage the disease makes its victims so unsightly that they must go masked. I am puzzled by the mutual sexual attraction of those in such a condition. I am also puzzled that the disease is not more contagious than it would appear to be, though of course the degree of contagion in the various forms of leprosy has always been uncertain.'

'Serjeant Jamieson?' said Cinquemani.

'Nothing to add,' said Jamieson, 'except that I admire the sensible practical dispositions which have been used to solve an embarrassing social problem.'

For some minutes we ate and drank without further discussion.

'And that is all,' said the Colonnello, 'that any of you have to say? You have noticed nothing more worthy of comment? You have not spotted the hiatus in all this history and explication? The hiatus which I am forbidden to indicate? The great question which I am forbidden to answer? Or even, in your presence, to ask?'

'I did say I was puzzled about certain things,' said Fotheringay.

'Minor matters. Sexual attraction between such unwholesome persons, for example. You surely know that if men and women are deprived of sexual relief for long enough they will satisfy themselves on almost anything. No, gentlemen. What you have missed is no such minor matter. There is one huge anomaly. You must search (on the strength of what you know already) and ye shall find. Knock hard enough and it shall be opened unto you. Or perhaps you think that you already know enough, and that from now on it will be safer and more agreeable to mind your own business, to look no further. If so, so be it. The choice is yours—the choice between knowledge and porcine acquiescence in ignorance.

'*Allora*,' the Colonnello concluded; 'now I must make my good-byes. I am to return to Padua sooner than I had thought.

I shall not see you again. Richard, *Ricardo* . . . dear friend of the Scuola di San Marco . . . I cannot dine with you as we had planned. For the rest of you, hail and farewell. *Addio*. I commend you all to God.'

'A few days later,' Adam told me in the Grill, 'I was summoned by the Comandante Corvino . . . to his office in the H.Q. of the Carabiniere near the Campiello del Vin. A very bare and dingy place it was: I had to squat on a bean-bag—all the furniture there was, except his chair and desk.'

'You need not have gone at all,' I said: 'as an Officer of the Forces of Occupation. . . .'

'Somehow one didn't feel like that with the Italians. Later on, with the Germans, one felt and behaved like an Occupying Power all right, and how one loved it. But the Italians were —well—frankly too childish and ridiculous. They gave the impression that if you carried on like an Army of Occupation they'd burst into tears.'

'They should have thought of that before they joined in the war with the Germans.'

'All the same,' said Adam, 'I didn't want to hurt Corvino's feelings; he'd been very helpful about getting us that flat in the Baldinucci; and anyhow I was anxious to find out what he had to say.'

'And what was that?'

'He said that the ten nurses from Marciume would be leaving the Palazzo in a few days. They would all be going on their hols, and then back to Marciume—but not via the Palazzo Baldinucci. He thought we'd be glad to know that we wouldn't be bothered with them any more, and that it would be months before any other parties on furlough came through for debriefing—by which time, he seemed to think, the British and Americans would have left Venice.'

'What made him think that?'

'Italian optimism. So I thanked him for the news and got off the bean-bag; and he civilly saw me down the stairs and

out on to the Riva degli Schiavoni. We were looking across at
San Giorgio Maggiore—there was a lowering sky that day, so
it looked like one of the more sinister Guardis—when he said
he'd thought of something else that might interest me.

' "Your friend, the Colonnello Cinquemani," he said: "you
knew 'e 'ad gone?"

' "Back to Padua, he told us."

'Corvino deliberately dropped both corners of his mouth,
a habit of his when he was passing on disturbing intelligence
which, he wished to make clear, one must know for one's good.

' "Not back to Padua, *caro Capitano*," Corvino said: "but into
an apartment in the Castle of the Island of Ustica. Near Sicily
... but since 1940 there is only one ferry a month. The thing
was, you see, that 'e got to know too much, about Marciume
and the pest and the patients—all that."

' "But surely," I said, "the more he knew the better. He was
investigating."

' " 'E was meant, *Signore*, to be studying the medical aspects
of the disease. No one asked 'im to investigate anything else."

' "Surely, he had to investigate everything connected with
the disease?"

' "Only up to a point. 'E 'ad passed that point. Doctor
Thrasymedes, the Master of the Ospedale degli Sognatori,
informed us that Cinquemani clearly knew something—
something 'physical' was Thrasymedes' word—that 'e ought
not to have known."

' " 'E did let on to us that there was more to all this than met
the eye. But he didn't say what. He said he was under a pledge to
be silent. Yet he urged us to work it out for ourselves. But as for
us, we had started to think that we knew more than enough for
our comfort already, without looking for further mysteries ...
of whatever kind."

' "Very sensible, *galante Capitano*," Corvino said: "just
you keep it that way. Think what 'as 'appened to Colonnello
Cinquemani. A warning to the curious."

'And of course now he had gone too far. Childish and ridiculous and rather *simpatico* the Italians might be, but when one of them got above himself, he had to be put in his place.

' "And just you remember, galante Comandante," I said, "what has happened to a number of your countrymen who have made themselves tiresome since the end of the war. I know you all try to pretend that you are really our allies, and we quite understand that many of you were not very keen on the Krauts, but if you threaten a British Officer you will have your trousers taken away, so to speak, and you will be stood in the Piazza for the public to pelt your *pudenda*. Am I plain?"

'Then he blinked in that silly way they have if they think they have been insulted. After a little,

' "You 'ave not understood," he said, ingratiating and pathetic. "You are not being threatened by me, or by the Carabiniere, or by the Secret Police—or by any Italian authority. As you say, it is not, just at present, within our power to do so. The threat, my friend, is knowledge. When Dottore Thrasymedes told me that Cinquemani knew too much, 'e was not encouraging us to take action on that account, 'e was predicting to us, for our reference, that something unpleasant might 'appen to the Colonel because of what 'e knew ... that *what 'e knew* would *of itself* injure or even destroy 'im. So do not ask me what instrument or agent removed the Colonel to 'is present quarters on Ustica; for to know that is part of the knowledge that could destroy you too. Just forget the whole matter."

' "Happily," I said, as the clouds drooped down on to San Giorgio Maggiore.'

But that turned out (Adam pursued) to be more easily said than done. Two days later Formosa appeared in the "Pox Poopers" Head Quarters, in order to say good-bye. She had not been there, nor been seen by any of them (except distantly on the terrace frequented by the nurses), since the first night of her arrival and her enticement of Richard Fotheringay. They had thought to have seen the last of her, and were now rather troubled by this visit of courtesy.

'I am now to thank you all for looking after me and being so kind on that night,' she said.

She was wearing the same kind of white overall as that in which she had disembarked a fortnight previously. She reached up to the neck, inserted her hand, fumbled in an inner pocket, and produced an envelope which she passed to Richard.

'*Caro Ricardo*,' she said, '*Ricardo caro*, I loved that night with you and wished there had been more. After I am gone, open that envelope for a memorial of me.'

'Not now, Formosa?'

'Not now, Ricardo.'

'Could we not meet? I understand that you have two weeks' holiday before you. I might get leave—'

'*Carissimo Ricardo*. Where I am going we cannot meet.'

'Is it to your parents, perhaps? Your parents, who would not like a British Officer . . . or any lover for their daughter?'

'Something of the kind.'

'Can I not . . . be with you before you go?'

'I wish you all to be with me before I go. Together. For fellowship. But it is a special thing. A dance. You will none of you take an actual part. You shall simply sit and watch.'

Formosa removed her overall, under which she was naked. Not only did she have pubes of Titian red, she had a narrow line of soft red hair running down from her breasts to her navel. She caressed these hairs as she started to sing:

> '*Quando il soave mio fido conforto*
> *per dar riposo a la mia vita stanca*
> *ponsi del letto in su la sponda manca. . . .*'

The tune to which she sang these words, and to which she now began to move in a slow, sinuous dance, resembled that of a hymn which Adam remembered from school, 'My Song is Love Unknown, My Saviour's Love for me, Love to the loveless shown. . . .' With a little squeezing here and expansion there, the Italian lines could be made to fit the tune quite naturally,

the rhythm of both being iambic. As Formosa danced, she mas-
turbated, deeply and copiously, with a small, smooth, bronze
statuette of a youth (either a Faun or a Bacchus?), which she had
taken from her overall as she discarded it.

> '*Tutto di pièta et di paura smorto,*' she sang, '*dico*;
> "*Onde vien tu ora, o felice alma?*" '

While her hips rotated, her thighs crossed, parted, slithered
together and crossed again; her little Bacchus (or Faun?) penetrated, frotted, withdrew and penetrated.

The three soldiers sat, still and stiff with lust. The song
murmured on, Formosa's fesses splayed and glutinously closed,
the Faun (or Bacchus?) mounted and descended, drenched by
the shining red labia. In the song a question was posed and an
answer given:

> ' "*Spirito ignudo sono e'n Ciel mi godo;*
> *quel che tu cerchi è terra gia molt' anni.*
> *Ma per trarti d'affani*
> *M' è dato a parer tale, et ancor quella*
> *sarò più che mai bella. . . .*" '

After these words Formosa arched her loins and jerked her
crotch towards the audience, fingering her now rampant clitoris
and at the same time thrusting the statuette with one long single
stroke into the depths of her vagina. For over two minutes her
head, neck and reins juddered with rhythmic violence. At last she
slowly withdrew the statuette, placed it on the floor at Richard's
feet, picked up her overall, and slipped away in absolute silence.

'For fellowship?' said Adam to me, pouring for both of us from
the decanter. 'What ever could she have meant?'

'That as a farewell gesture, and to show her gratitude, she
wished to give you pleasure by this remarkable exhibition of
herself.'

'That was what we assumed,' said Adam. 'We examined the things she had left behind her. First, the statuette: undeniably of Bacchus or a close associate, because he had his head back to guzzle at a bunch of grapes; probably a copy made in the 2nd Century A.D. from a much earlier original.

'Who told you that?'

'A Senior Curator of the Accademia, a day or two later. Not that the date mattered very much, but the identification with Bacchus or a member of his gang was interesting when one remembered that the earliest sufferers from the pest had brought it back from Naxos and were supposed to have contracted it from a Spring which Bacchus had cursed.'

'Not that that would get you very far. In any case,' I said, 'I understood that you had stopped sticking your noses into all that in response to Corvino's warning.'

'So we had. But Formosa's behaviour did seem to require a little explanation ... particularly,' said Adam, 'after we had seen what was in the envelope which she had left for Richard Fotheringay as a "memorial". It was a copy, in what one presumed was her own handwriting, of a long Italian poem which included the words which she had sung during her act.'

'What was the poem about?'

'I'm sorry to say that we had no idea. So I decided to take it to Comandante Corvino, who should be able to translate it (though the language did seem rather dated). I could then find out whether the strange manner of Formosa's *congé* would in any way modify his command to mind our own business. You see, it did seem that Formosa was trying to leave us some kind of message—in which case it might be our business after all.'

So Adam had repaired to the Carabinieri H.Q. on the Riva degli Schiavoni, handed the Comandante the paper which Formosa had left, explained how it had been acquired, and sat down on a bean-bag to hear what Corvino made of it.

'This is Petrarch,' said Corvino almost at once: 'I was made to read 'im in School. One of a set of poems called the *Rime Sparse*. One of 'is *Canzoni*.'

'What's it all about?'

'If you are an Officer of the Forces occupying Venice, you ought to 'ave learnt enough of our language, *galante Capitano*, to know what it's about.'

'It is a difficult poem, *galante Comandante*, in an archaic idiom.'

Corvino turned down the corners of his mouth. 'Un'ealthy poetry,' he said. 'This Petrarch, 'e imagine that 'is mistress, Laura, long dead, 'as come to sit by 'im on 'is bed. She 'as come to comfort 'im. But 'e wants too much comfort, so she tells 'im she is a vision, a vision come to tell 'im how lovely it is to be in 'eaven, and 'ow she 'opes 'e'll be joining her there 'imself one time. And to take 'is lustful 'ands off her, because that dainty flesh 'e's fancying 'as long since turned to dust ... *è terra mult' anni*. And now she's got to go back to the angels, but she'll come again soon, gold 'air, big tits and all, to tell 'im that the spirit is all that really matters—teasy-weasy, as your soldiers say—and to make sure 'e's concentrating on 'is salvation. 'E must remember that she is only allowed to look so sexy in order to get 'is atten-tion to what she is saying about 'is soul—'is soul, 'is soul. But for all she keep saying this, Petrarch try one last pass and Laura tells 'im 'e is a dirty pig—the exact words are left to imagine, words that "could break the bones" Petrarch says—and then 'e wake up crying. Why,' enquired the Commandant, 'are some of the lines marked in pencil?'

'That was us. They are the lines we think we heard her sing-ing while she was carrying on with the statuette.'

'Well, these lines 'ere are when Petrarch is asking what she's doing in 'is bed,' said Corvino, rapping the paper. 'Come round and stand 'ere. . . .' Adam came round and stood ' 'ere' and looked down on an immaculate index finger, with a short nail neatly filed into an elegant curve, as it pointed at the lines beginning '*Tutto di pièta et di paura smorto*'. ' "All pale with rev-erence and fear",' said Corvino, ' 'e asks where she's come from and why she's there. She tells 'im, she's come from 'eaven' to make sure 'e's a good boy and fit to go there 'imself. 'E says, "it's your body I want" or words to that effect, and she replies, at this marked passage, "*Spirito ignudo sono*", I'm really a naked spirit and I rejoice in 'eaven. I've already told you the rest.'

'So it seems,' said Adam, 'that Formosa was taking both parts —both Petrarch and Laura. What do we deduce from that?'

'We deduce nothing from that,' said Corvino, 'because we 'ave already agreed to forget the whole thing. She told the three of you she was saying "good-bye", so good-bye let it be.'

'She also seems to be saying—in that song—that she might come back again. Was that her last message to us, do you think?'

'For your sake,' said Corvino, 'I sincerely trust not. You'll get no good of 'er, nor any of the rest of them. That much I can tell you . . . my dear Adam.'

'But if she should come back . . . my dear Piero?'

'What would they 'ave told you to do, at your Eton Academy and your Sandhurst College?'

'Play it by eye and by ear.'

'Good advice, my friend, as far as it goes. Though whether "play" is the right *parola* I am very uncertain.'

'So then,' said Adam to me, pouring again from the decanter, 'Serjeant Jamieson, Lieutenant Fotheringay, and myself held a Council of War, sitting on the marble bench above the little dell and the prancing Satyr.

' "In her desire for sex," said Richard, "Formosa resembles Petrarch."

' "In her hint that she will return," said Richard, "she resembles Laura."

' "In her sexual performance," I said, "both in public before the three of us and in private with Richard (as he tells the tale) she resembles a very desperate woman."

' "Easily explicable," said Richard, "on that first night, when she had just returned from that horrible island."

' "And easily explicable," said Jamieson, "on that second and last visit, if she did not like the idea of where she was going next. She was pretty vague about that."

' "Wherever she was going next," said Richard, "we know that she was ultimately to rejoin her friends and return to Marciume. That alone might make any sane person desperate."

' " 'For fellowship'," I quoted Formosa herself. "All right, she liked us, she wanted to give us pleasure before saying goodbye, but somehow none of this quite fits the deep, human need of the phrase 'for fellowship'. Tell me: do you two want to go on with this after all, despite Corvino's warning?"

' "Yes," said Richard the young man, the student of human kind.

' "Why not let us wait," said the more cautious Jamieson (who had a wife and son in England), "until she comes back . . . *if* she comes back?"

' "We may be gone by then," I said (I, who was also young then): "time and chance work very quickly in war and its immediate aftermath."

' "True," said Jamieson; "and I do want to know how it all works . . . whatever 'it' may be."

' "Then you are both with me?" I said.

' "Sir," said Jamieson, reverting to the Guardsman, short back and sides, eyes to the front, Captain my Captain.

' "Upon the honour of a man of science," Fotheringay said.

' "Very well," I said. "I see, now, only one possible course. I shall go to Thrasymedes again and find out what he knew and what he knows of Francesco Cinquemani." '

So the next morning Adam went through the Campo Lamorea and the Campo di Naxos, crawled the length of the tunnel into the Campo degli Sognatori, mounted the stair in front of the Ospedale, knocked on the door with the early Gothic Arch, and was received, if not welcomed, by Doctor Thrasymedes. Thrasymedes was in laboratory whites but this time he wore no turban; the upper half of his head was much shorter and narrower, Adam now saw, than the lower, giving him a pyramidal appearance on the top storey.

'Tell me, Dottore Thrasymedes,' Adam said immediately, 'what has become of our friend, the Colonnello Cinquemani?'

Thrasymedes nodded, assumed an expression of sour resignation, and signed to Adam to follow. He then led him out of the hallway, into the Museum, past the clinical and forensic exhibits in their glass cases and tanks, and then to the right down a brief, dark corridor. At the end of this he unlocked a bronze-studded door.

'The Muniments Room,' he said.

On the walls to the left and at either end were racks of torn and tilted books; on the floor and on one large central table (like the Dining Table of an important Officers' Mess, long enough for at least fifteen diners on either side) were piles of paper, parchment and yellow newsprint. Over all was a deep stench of vegetable decay.

'As I told you and your friends the other day,' said Thrasymedes, 'most of the contents of this room are rotted to pieces or indecipherable. But one of two of the stouter or more recent volumes are exceptions.'

He turned to a shelf near the door, pulled down a green volume of 24 inches by nine by three thick, and carried it to the sill of a long window on his right, the only window, which looked down on the Campo degli Sognatori.

'Cinquemani wrote me a letter,' said Thrasymedes. He rested the green volume, still closed, on the sill in front of him. 'He wrote it on the evening of the day you all came here—the evening before he left. He said that I might be interested in a conversation which he had had in the Palazzo Baldinucci with one of the male attendants or nurses from Marciume, a man he named as Marcello, the so called Caporale in charge of the medical team. This conversation had nothing to do with the lepers on the island or with Marcello's duties towards them; it was concerned solely with the welfare of Marcello and his colleagues. One brief quotation:

' " "We respect the capacities,' " Cinquemani reported Marcello as saying, " 'of the Doctors and Psychiatrists who come here to examine us after our tours of duty on Marciume. On the whole they take excellent care of our physical and mental condition. Our spiritual difficulties are not so well provided for; it would almost seem that because of our special status it is thought that the attentions of a priest would be otiose or inappropriate. But in truth it is just that special status that makes us long for somebody to regard us, not only as flesh and blood and brain, but also as souls that aspire to the love of God their Creator. We yearn for spiritual fellowship.' "

'Spiritual fellowship?' muttered Adam. And then, 'What did Marcello mean by "special status"?'

'That is what the Colonnello wished to find out. But Marcello told him only that he and his colleagues were members of a congregation that conferred that status, as if they made up some kind of college or religious order.'

'In that case,' said Adam, 'why should they require a priest from outside?'

'Once again, this was just the kind of thing which interested the Colonnello ... now that the topic had been raised. In his letter to me, Cinquemani says that when he started to question Marcello along these lines, Marcello was evasive. However, he did suggest to the Colonel that the only way he could truly understand the problem of the Caporale and his companions was to visit the team—"fellowship" was the word used once more—during the period of leisure which they would enjoy before going back to Marciume. For they do not go on separate holidays, as the official version would imply, but they go together to one of several asylums or sanctuaries.'

'In this case, the Island of Ustica?'

'Yes. The Island of Ustica, north of Sicily. There, said Cinquemani in his letter, he was now going himself. He could not tell you because of his oath, but he could tell me because I was officially involved. I think he wanted it known to you and your friends. I decided that it was not my affair to tell you unless you specifically enquired ... as indeed you now have.'

'You told Corvino.'

'He too is officially involved. I had to warn him that Cinquemani might be in danger.'

'Corvino,' said Adam, 'saw fit to tell me where Cinquemani had gone. He indicated that some terrible fate might be in store for him, and urged, not for the first time, that I should have nothing whatever to do with it all from that moment on. Cinquemani, on the other hand, has been ambivalent. He did not tell us, yet you say he wanted us to know. He revealed a great deal to us but not his destination—nor his conversation with Marcello. Can you explain his ambiguity?'

'He was fond of you all. Although he hoped you would deduce the whole truth eventually, he did not wish you to take risks. Or again: by not telling you his destination straight away but leaving it possible that you might find out, he ensured that by the time you followed him—if you did so—he would be in a position to protect you.'

'In short,' said Adam, 'his own knowledge is very far from complete. What do you know of these risks, of the horrors hinted at by Corvino, which apparently attach to Ustica?'

'Nothing at all. My duty is to concoct suitable medicaments for the patients on Marciume, not to concern myself with the personal or social problems of their nurses. But I have been considering, with interest and informed speculation, one particular item in this book.' He held up the green volume. 'One item that you might find relevant if you too wish to go to Ustica.'

'You would not object?'

'It is not my place to object. I should, of course, tell the Comandante Corvino. For your own sakes.'

'Ustica, after all these years of war, has become very remote. There are few ferries and endless official obstacles to travel.'

'A Captain of Military Police ought to be able to overcome them.'

'What is the item in that book which I might find relevant?'

'It is an edition of 1630 of Strabo's *Geography of the Roman World*,' said Doctor Thrasymedes, opening it. 'It is written in Greek but with maps by the hand of the Venetian scholar Paulo

Paulus, *floruit* 1628. Strabo points out . . . here . . . that Ustica is almost due north of Palermo—Panormus as it was called in his day. Paulo's map confirms this.'

'I need neither Strabo nor Paulus come from the grave to tell me *that*,' said Adam.

'Perhaps you did not understand—as Strabo will remind you—that in climate and soil Ustica is in many ways similar to Palermo. Just as Sicily has a volcanic soil, so has Ustica.'

'And so, Dottore?'

'Just as Palermo has a rich soil and very dry air, so has Ustica.'

'Be plain.'

'There are also cultural similarities. For example, persecution of the early Christians by the Roman administration.'

'A common phenomenon. Be plainer.'

'Early Christians who were persecuted hid themselves in catacombs . . . a traditional refuge of unpopular sects . . . or of people whom an ignorant population might regard as being sinister in some way . . . carrying contagious diseases perhaps.'

'Why should Marcello and the rest go all the way to Ustica for sanctuary?'

'That is what Cinquemani has gone to find out. He has gone there voluntarily, whatever else Corvino may have hinted at in order to frighten you and deter your curiosity.'

'Corvino spoke of Cinquemani . . . as I told you . . . as being under some appalling threat of evil—not posed by the Italian authorities but somehow connected with the lepers and Marciume and the nurses and even, I suppose, with this Hospital.'

'This Ospedale poses no threats,' Thrasymedes said.

'Then what does?'

'That,' said Thrasymedes for the second time, 'is what Cinquemani has gone to find out.'

'So,' said Adam over the port, 'the H.Q. of the Pox Poopers went into administrative conference.' The two furrows, which ran from either corner of his nostrils to either corner of his mouth, were becoming deeper as the night went on. 'How should we get to Ustica? And which of us should remain behind to license and control our pretty girls and boys in Venice?

'It was a difficult decision. Serjeant Jamieson was the obvious man to keep the shop in Venice, but his logistic skills might be valuable over the length of what was still virtually war-time Italy. And anyhow we ought to leave a Commissioned Officer in charge of our H.Q. Richard Fotheringay could, at a pinch, administer as well as provide medical care and inspection; but he might be useful in Ustica because of his influence over For-mosa. Perhaps I myself should stay behind? But a commander's place is in the front line. In the end, it was determined that all three of us must go; Serjeant Jamieson was deputed to use the Serjeants' and Warrant Officers' network to find somebody who could stand in for us at the Palazzo Baldinucci. He came up with the ideal solution: a knobby old ranker Captain who had just survived a Court Martial for dealing on the Black Market, and his oppo, a Medical Orderly with the rank of Corporal who had handled the Drugs department of the enterprise and had wormed his way through a parallel Court Martial. Both were awaiting posting home but had no priority of any kind; the O.C. movements (or rather, his O.R.Q.M.S. on his behalf) was happy to assure us, in return for a small contribution towards the "Near Eastern Forces' Welfare Fund", that this delightful pair would not be posted anywhere for at least six weeks. In return for a rather more substantial contribution to an even more vaguely specified fund, our chosen delegates, Captain "Snouty" Footcock (lately Q.M. to the 13th Battalion of the South East Middlesex Regiment) and Sergeant "Clappy" Manifold of the R.A.M.C. graciously condescended to take on the functions of the Pox Poopers for four weeks plus odd days (at extra emolu-ment) if necessary. The Brigadier Commandant of the Military Police in Trentino-Veneto was absent on his second consecutive month of compassionate leave in Rome, and his deputy was disinclined to interfere with arrangements made by myself, who regularly sent him the pick of the season's tapettes on approval. Our expedition, or at least our absence, had therefore received prompt and official blessing; and on a fair summer's morning we departed for Ravenna-San Marino-Firenze-Roma-Napoli-Amalfi-Scilla-Palermo in a Staff Colonel's Car, procured by Jamieson from a Company Sergeant-Major in the Motor Pool at the Piazzale Roma, along with field Petrol coupons enough to cover the return journey to Palermo five times ('We can sell the surplus,' Jamieson said, 'to recompense us for bribes and expenses'), as a measure of the C.S.M.'s gratitude for being provided with some sexual delicacy in the sub-Lolita category.

' "Pity we're not just going sight-seeing," said Fotheringay as we turned south from Mestre: "there are lots of things on our way which I long to see. Any hope of stopping at Paestum for an hour or two?"

' "The people we are going to meet," I said, "probably won't be there for more than a fortnight. There may be horrible problems getting from Palermo to Ustica. I fear lest I must be stern about our priorities."

' "Right you be," said Fotheringay; "perhaps on the way back? If the driver doesn't mind."

' "Speaking as your driver, gentlemen," said Serjeant Jamieson, "I don't mind anything except incivility or complaint."

' "You will be offered neither," I said.

' "Not from you two, sir. From official busybodies further south. So kindly sign this work ticket for me." He passed back a millboard with a complicated document attached. "The chief signatory, as you will notice, sir, is a household name."

' "How on earth did you manage that?"

' "The Squadron Corporal-Major in charge of the Mess for his personal entourage received a large consignment of fresh caviar and high quality vodka. Such favours require recognition. The S.C.M. persuaded the General that the suppliers needed a long holiday after their exertions. The General is well known to be a nobleman of liberal habit."

' "Why must I countersign?"

' "The vehicle is on your charge, sir. Total anonymity I could not achieve."

'What a joy that journey was,' said Adam to me, pouring the last of the port. 'The war over, everyone in a happy temper, the fields smiling and the sun shining, the country lads and lasses brimming with juice and roses, the wrack and ruin of battle merely a poetic, a theoretical reminder of mortality. No trouble anywhere, no need even to produce the General's signature, for the presence of a doctor rendered our progress far too serious to be questioned. An easy crossing from Scilla to Charybdis, a spectacular drive along the North Coast of Sicily to Palermo ... where we garaged the Staff Car and exchanged some of our Petrol Coupons for swift private passage to Ustica. But then ...'

'Then what?' I said.

Adam Ogilvie, Richard Fotheringay and Serjeant Jamieson were greeted, at the little port under the fortress, by Colonnello Francesco Cinquemani.

'Thrasymedes wired me you was coming,' he said; 'I have been waiting for your arrival. Since you have disregarded all the advice you have been given you deserve to be left on your own to suffer whatever might come your way. However ... I have eaten your salt, that is, I have drunk your wine in your garden ... and so I shall be your guide. I shall show you all that is to be shown, and tell you all that is to be told, and throughout I shall be not only your guide but guard—on this one condition: that when you have been shown and when you have been told, you shall leave this place immediately; that you make no criticism, no judgment, and above all no attempt to interfere. Only when you are clear of Ustica and clear of Sicily will you begin to evaluate or assess.'

'I am a doctor, I have certain obligations—' Richard Fotheringay began.

'—I too am a doctor. I tell you that here you have none.'

'Very well,' said Richard.

'Any other objections?' Cinquemani said.

Adam and Jamieson exchanged glances and shook their heads.

'Then follow me.'

Cinquemani led them along a narrow street (Adam continued his tale) between houses on each side that nearly touched at the top. Cords were slung across the gap; quaint garments were hung to dry from them, as from the lines in the Ghetto in Venice, red and yellow and green. At some stage the tops of the houses came so close together that the four men were now in what was almost a tunnel; then the houses ceased to be houses and turned into the steep sides and tapering vault of what was indeed a tunnel. Cinquemani and his followers advanced towards total dark; Cinquemani produced two torches.

'With one I shall light the way. With the other you, *Ricardo mio*, shall bring up in the rear, lighting the path for yourself and your friends between you and me.'

The tunnel became broader, then, as the roof descended, elliptical. The path under their feet was a yard wide and very dry, almost, it seemed, as if baked by fire. It began to ascend, rather sharply. To their right was a stream running parallel to the path. Fotheringay shone his torch on it; such was the filth which it was carrying down past them, the ordure and the broken red flesh, that he immediately turned the torch away and back to the path in front of him. There was, however, no stink, no stench, no smell whatever.

'Refuse from the castle sewer and the kitchens,' said Cinquemani. 'Like Dante and Virgil we are on a path ascending through the earth with a stream beside it. The only differences are that Dante's stream was pure, and that, whereas Dante and Virgil were ascending away from Hell, we are ascending towards it.'

And on they went. Sometimes, when the gradient became unusually steep, the path was interrupted by a flight of steps, seldom more than ten or fifteen. The steps were of stone, the path continued to be of baked soil.

'In the fortress,' said the Colonnello, 'is a small garrison of allied troops guarding a handful of German prisoners. The stream, as I have said, is a primitive means of disposing of the waste from the kitchens and hygienic installations—such as they are. These are in the basement of the castle. Beneath this basement, well beneath it, is a set of—'

'—Catacombs?' Adam said. 'Or so Thrasymedes seemed to think.'

'Catacombs,' confirmed the Colonnello.

'Like the ones under Palermo?'

'Pretty well. They have the same dehydrated air. Even drier, in fact.'

The path began to slope more gently, then became nearly level. It turned away from the filthy yet odourless stream.

'Dry air modifies decay and therefore reduces stench,' the Colonel said. 'Like Dante and Virgil we shall soon come to "*un pertugio tondo*", a "round opening",' he continued; 'but unlike them we shall not emerge under the stars.'

They emerged, in fact, into a square-sectioned and orderly corridor (the "roundness" disappearing a few yards after they had left the uphill tunnel), the walls and ceiling of which were copiously whitewashed.

'The whiteness will help you to see,' said Cinquemani: 'we shall now halt for a few minutes to let you get your breath and to prepare you for the remainder of the journey. To put us all in good heart we shall sing a song. Now, what shall it be? Something robust, to fortify us, yet not over-confident, lest we should irritate the gods of the underworld by our presumption. Ah; I know: a soldiers' song. A favourite song of your own British soldiers, which sometimes they sing in the fortress above:—

' "We don't know where we're going till we're there," ' he sang;

    ' "Round and round and round the barrack square;
        We heard the Sergeant say,
         'We're on the move to-day',
    But he never really told us how or where." '

'So—all together now—"We don't know where we're

going till we're there"—*quick march*—"Round and round and round the barrack square ..." '

Colonel Cinquemani led off down the whitewashed corridor, his little band of three followed in Indian file. They rounded a corner and saw ahead what looked like a changing room, rows of pegs on the left hand side of the corridor, with long clothes dangling from them, white overalls as they shortly discovered, with the Caporale Marcello and Formosa and their eight comrades inside them, hanging from strong black wooden pegs, not by nooses but in halters which passed under their arms. Their faces were chalk white, their bodies totally inert, their eyes open and sightless, looking straight out unseeing at the gawping Pox Poopers, whose silly song gurgled and ceased like the strangled organ (Daisy, Daisy) of a dying roundabout in the September rain.

'Ten corpses,' said Adam to me in the Grill Room, 'ten white cadavers hanging on a wall ... which (or who), as Francesco now made plain, would wake up. Quite soon. And we'd all better be gone when they did so because in the chagrin of waking from their rest they were capable of being very disagreeable to intruders. . . .'

Nevertheless, the Colonel had given no immediate word to move. 'Very dry air, you see,' the Colonel said to Adam and Co. in the corridor, 'preserves corpses. Here as in Palermo. Did you ever visit the catacombs there before the war? No. Adam and Ricardo would have been too young; and before the war—forgive me, Serjeant—British Other Ranks, even from the Brigade of Guards, did not travel into Europe. So let me tell you about those catacombs below Palermo. There is a perfectly preserved baby—the sort of baby that makes women go "Aaaaah"—who has been there since 1867. And a Cardinal in full red robes, both prelate and finery slightly shrunk but otherwise full of grace and eminence, hanging from the highest hook in the place of pride. The air in the catacombs here in Ustica is believed to be even more efficacious in this regard. What better place for the undead to rest until they come alive again, suitably renewed for another stint of the horrible, selfless labours which they must endure, with periods of joyless recuperation, for ever?'

He paused for this to sink in.

'Jacobo Messalino,' he said, 'the first Master of the Ospedale degli Sognatori, gave the lepers an elixir which kept them, on the whole, quiet and orderly. Even so, their numbers gradually increased—more were born than died—and, as you know, some 250 years after the foundation of the Ospedale its inhabitants had to be transferred to the more ample quarters which were made available on the Island of Marciume. But there was then a problem. People who were prepared to do the wretched job of nursing these repellent (if pathetic) patients in Venice itself were not prepared to be confined with them on a dank and dismal islet, which was little better than a bank of mud, in the outer regions of the Lagoon. The Master of the Ospedale was compelled to search for new recruits for the task. He was growing more and more frantic when a man named Marcello came to him and told him that he was the leader of an itinerant band of priests and priestesses from Egypt. They had been expelled from Alexandria for some violation of sectarian law, and had now formed an independent group. They were, he said, in search of God's peace through penitence, service and suffering, and the task of minding a more than usually foul species of leper would be just what they needed. There were twenty of them; he suggested to the Master that—should he find them fit for the office—they should be divided into two sections of ten persons, working turn and turn about, a period with the lepers on Marciume, then a period of prayer and meditation on the nearby islet of Tetro. The full twenty postulants would manage the move of the colony from Venice to Marciume, would refurbish the broken church and the ruined dwellings which had been left by the former inhabitants of Marciume and Tetro, and would proceed with matters from thereon. The Master of the Ospedale could continue with medical research—a pleasant occupation of small practical value (as the thing was at that time conducted)—and would not be disturbed by Marcello except in case of crisis or acute need of emergency provisions.

'The grateful Master accepted the offer with the bare minimum of enquiry, and felt himself to have been justified when the evacuation of the lepers to Marciume was conducted without one single hitch by the calm and competent Marcello, assisted by his nineteen sectaries. After about a month Marcello returned briefly to the Ospedale, and confirmed that everything was now in place: the system of shifts was in smooth operation, and his brothers and sisters were well satisfied with their work on Marciume and their leisure on Tetro for prayer and self-abasement before God. Finally, said Marcello, the Master should understand that the agreed payment to his Order for their services should be deposited with a well known Jew Banker at his place of business near the Rialto. And how, asked the Master, would Marcello acquire new recruits to carry on the contract when the number of his Order began to fail through sickness or death? The Order, Marcello replied, consisted of equal numbers of either sex: thus it could be recruited through natural propagation to replace the wastage of time. The Order would see to all that. Very well, said the Master: but if ever the numbers of the Order fell below a certain level, Marcello should inform the Master of the day and request assistance. Marcello bowed and withdrew, and was not heard of again. Indeed nothing more was heard from Marciume or Tetro for well over two hundred years—nothing, that is, apart from routine application for, and acknowledgment of, basic foods, stores and medicaments. After five years there was an end even of this exchange. It was understood that Marcello had rendered his two miserable islands self-supporting, by means of agriculture and the growth of herbs on Tetro, which, being unvisited by the lepers, had earth and air pure enough for the purpose.

'One day in the early 18th Century the then Master of the Ospedale was inquisitive enough to visit the successor of the Jew Banker nominated by Marcello. He was told that monies deposited over the years by the Plague Chest of the Serenissima for the credit of the Order of Penitents of Alexandria, together with the compound interest which had accrued (and was of course still accruing at an ever more rapid rate) now amounted, in round figures, to twenty-two and a half million ducats. It was at this point that the Order, the Islands and the Lepers of Naxos (the Sognatori), for 250 years out of sight and out of mind, began to attract official attention.'

The Colonnello now led Adam and his men away from the rank of suspended corpses and up, through the kitchens, into the castle.

'Accommodation is prepared,' said the Colonnello. 'You will stay this night only. We shall all dine together—and in the morning you shall sail back to Palermo and leave, *instanter*, for Venice.'

'We dined by candlelight,' Adam told me, 'in Colonel Cinquemani's quarters, which had once been those of the Bourbon Governor. It seemed that a high status was conferred, though by whom was not quite clear, on the man who would greet and soothe the nurses on their awakening, always a difficult time, and see them back to relieve the other sectaries on Marciume. But this is to anticipate. Let me revert to the Colonel's discourse . . .'

Dinner was served (Adam pursued) by Italian Orderlies. As soon as they had handed the main course (stewed octopus), Francesco Cinquemani began to dilate:

'We shall not be disturbing you on our return journey to Marciume,' said Francesco Cinquemani, 'though you may be seeing us later on. Indeed the probability of this is so strong that I must now tell you rather more about the Order of Penitents of Alexandria and their code of behaviour.

'Now, I was saying to you that in the early 18th Century the Order attracted attention in Venice, for the first time in centuries, because of the size of its Bank Balance. This led to an official investigation of the affairs of the Ospedale, of its relation with the Directors of the Ospedale, of its relation with the Directors of the Plague Chest (whom old Master Jacobo Messalino had persuaded to fund it *sine die*), and of the two islands nominally in its care. Since several members of the Council required sinecures for nephews and so forth, it was decided to form an Inspectorate of the Islands: five Inspectors, to be liberally paid from the accumulated wealth of the Order itself, would make monthly visits. In the course of time the monthly visits became annual (there was, after all, never anything at fault) and the annual visits were reduced to one every five years and then to every ten. A very Venetian proceeding. However, it was eventually noticed by one long-lived Inspector that in the entire sixty years since his appointment nobody at all, among the two teams of nurses, had changed. All of them looked exactly the same; none of them appeared to have died and certainly none had been born. Seeing no cause to trouble his fellow Inspectors with this circumstance, the octogenarian Marco Caffetier (*Nobilis Homo*) took the Chief of the Order (Marcello) on one side and apologetically remarked (so it is related in the Secret Annals of the Serenissima):

' "There would seem, my dear—er—Father Marcello—to be no difference in yourself nor in any of your brothers and sisters since first I encountered you on these islands well over half a century ago. I am not one to raise unnecessary complaints, the less so as your care of these unfortunate lepers or whatever is so tireless and skilful, but I am slightly curious as to your—er—unusual durability."

'As Caffetier subsequently wrote in his report for the Secret Annals, Father Marcello was not in the least offended by the enquiry but addressed his inquisitor as follows:

' "I have often wondered, Signor Ispettore, when this question would be asked, and I have given much thought to my answer. Know, then, that the Order of the Penitents of Alexandria was previously called the Order of the Guardians of Epidaurus, since it originated in the Temple there. You will recall that the great physician Asclepius brought back to life the dead Hippolytus—and was damned and slain by the King of the Gods for his presumption. You will also recollect that Hippolytus was not only brought back to life but henceforth became immortal; he was taken by the Goddess Diana to live with her by Lake Nemi. Asclepius then, though now dead himself, had had the gift of conferring eternal life on the dead—a gift he had passed on to his favourite pupil, Asclepiades, during his incumbency at Epidaurus. Asclepiades, hearing of his master's triumph with Hippolytus, determined to create from bodies dead at Epidaurus a number of Immortals as a Memorial to the dead Asclepius. These were twenty in number—myself and my nineteen brothers and sisters, who now tend the sick, as we were taught to at Epidaurus, as our destiny for ever and for ever. At first we practised at Epidaurus itself, where we were visited by those who suffered from all over the world; and then, when ejected by busybodying Christians in the 7th Century A.D., we travelled to many places—to Athens, Rome, Ravenna, Taranto and Alexandria, always exercising our beneficent skills, always in the end expelled by spies and bigots, who disapproved of what you so politely call our 'durability'. That is why we insisted on payment for our work here—only so that we should have ample resources to move elsewhere when we were, eventually, rejected."

'"But you will not be rejected by Venice," said the stout Marco Caffetier (*N.H.*): "you are far too useful. But I fear we shall somehow have to place your office and your status on a more regulated level. Not everyone in Venice is as tolerant as I am. So before anyone else discovers your unusual condition and starts to be censorious about it, I shall have you renamed as the Order of Immortals, registered as such, engaged and salaried as such. Such is the official mind, you see, that if once a name or title is accepted and allotted, those described by it will not only be allowed but positively commanded to display the substance and attributes which it conveys. Named as the Order of Immortals, you will be explained, respected and provided for as immortal, this being thenceforth your official state and style and carrying no præternatural, anomalous, perverted or malignant connotation. This should lead to considerable improvement in the arrangement of your lives—if you will forgive the term; for once you are bureaucratically acknowledged as what you are we shall be able to provide suitable accommodation, holidays and so on. What we must never do, of course, is inform the general public about you, as the masses, in their ignorance, stupidity and cowardice, would be unremittingly hostile. The upper classes, even the administrative classes, will show you only appreciation and gratitude; they know a good thing when they see it: but your secret must never be revealed to the jacquerie."

' "We are used to prejudice," said Father Marcello, "but would certainly wish to rouse none, as it is an obstacle to our work. You referred to improved accommodation and holidays. These things mean little to us. We exist for our vocation— though one or two things might be done to enable us to enjoy more convenient places and periods of rest and renewal: even our perennial flesh should on occasion be given respite."

' "Any request will be quickly met," said Marco; "you and I will confer at length later. Meanwhile, good father, am I really to believe that you had your origins as a corpse under the hands of a priest at Epidaurus? The explanation is witty, but not wholly convincing."

' "The explanation is a myth, Signor Ispettore. Like all myths it explains satisfactorily and poetically why things are as they are, without necessarily being true. Do not, I must ask you, seek to enquire further."

' "My dear father, of course not. Forgive me if I have embarrassed you. But one final question: I quite understand that you exist for your work and derive great satisfaction from it; but do you never desire anything else to entice your minds and pleasure your bodies?"

' "We seek for a God, Signore, whom we cannot find. In his place we yearn for fellowship with Mankind. Fellowship of

mind and body. Both are rare. Fellowship of mind we sometimes find with one such as yourself: Fellowship of body, very
occasionally with some wanderer among the islands of the
Lagoon. For we know desire; and though we strive to couple
with each other, we are long since—long centuries since—sick
of each other's stale bodies. Nor can we beget children on each
other—though sometimes, as when we first came to Venice, we
falsely pretend that we can, in order to disarm suspicion about
the continuance of our number.... We *desire*, Signore, but the
vigour in us is roused only by humankind."

' "Then could you beget children with mortal men or
women?"

' "No. That was ... disordained by Asclepiades lest we should
beget (or bear) a race of half-breeds, neither mortal nor immortal. Who knows what such children might turn into? For that
matter, who knows what children we might have had if we had
been able to breed on one another? But what we might beget on
mortals, Signore, is love in ourselves and love in them."

' "What about the poor creatures whom you succour?"

' "With them there can be no Fellowship save that of
pity. Their minds are clouded by their disease, their bodies
spoiled."

' "We might find you human company, both of mind and
body," said Marco, "among the arrangements we shall make."

' "No," said Father Marcello wearily. "You see, in order to
maintain this secrecy you rightly regard as essential—to keep
news of our nature from the rabble—we have long found it
necessary to ... dispose finally ... of any human being who
comes close enough to us to realise that we are the undead."

' "The wanderers in the islands?"

' "Yes, if they came to know too much. Most did not."

' "So ... while you yearn for fellowship ... if this becomes
too close, you must kill what you love and what loves you?"

' "Yes. Ironic, is it not?"

' "I imagine then," said Marco, "that you must now finally
dispose of me?"

' "Luckily your advanced age, Signor Ispettore, will enable us to dispense with your disposal."

' "But no renaming you as Immortals, I think?"

' "No," said Marcello.

' "I shall have to do what I can for you, in the short time that remains to me, without letting anyone into your secret."

' "If you please, Signore. It is only because your time must be so very short—for it is clear to me with my millennia of medical practice that you may have a fatal stroke at any second—that we shall permit you to continue."

' "You trust *nobody*?"

' "Nobody. Not even the upper or administrative classes," said Marcello with a tight smile. "No one who understands the wonder and enormity of our predicament can be trusted not to betray us. That has been made very plain to us since we left Epidaurus a thousand years ago."

' "You are right, of course. How would you go about finally disposing of me, did not my extreme infirmity make this unnecessary?"

' "We should give you a draught. Your death would not be painful. Even so, I am glad it will not fall to me to promote it."

' "Thank you, dear father Marcello." '

'All of which,' said Adam to me, idly dangling the empty decanter, 'posed a significant question. By this time, Fotheringay, Jamieson and I knew all about the Order of the Guardians of Epidaurus and their immortal life and function—or quite enough to merit our disposal. By Marcello's measure, we were a threat to the Order's security. However, did Marcello and his brothers and sisters realise this? And if not, could we reasonably hope to go free? One began to understand, all too painfully, the force behind Corvino's warnings and Cinquemani's. And yet Cinquemani had more or less tempted us to persist in our search. Was he confident that he could protect us? Or had he merely become so tired of our importunity that he was resigned to giving us our heads and leaving us to whatever fate might come of it? Had he not spoken of future visits from himself and members of the Order ("You may be seeing us later on")? What did he mean by that?'

'Did you not ask?' I said. 'After all, the Colonnello Cinquemani was your friend; although he had, as you say, warned you against poking your noses in, he had also encouraged you. When you arrived in Ustica, he had, without further ado, taken you to the heart of the matter and made it all as plain as such a weird affair ever could be. So whatever his motives, whatever his intentions, past, present or future, he owed it to you to come clean.'

'Oh, he came clean all right,' Adam said. 'He told us that in our case, provided Marcello and the rest never knew we had seen them as they "recuperated" in the catacombs, all would be well. Their corpses were not due to awaken till later the next day. The apprehension which he had whipped up when we first saw the hanging cadavers, he said, was mere showmanship. Let us be gone at dawn, and no harm would have been done.

'And future intercourse with the brothers and sisters,' Adam had persisted. 'Cinquemani himself had said not only that this might occur but that it was "probable". He had also told us how to deal with this, Cinquemani replied, by giving detail of their customs and their yearnings. If they came to us from Marciume for Fellowship of Mind or Body, we must simply take care we did not come too close to them or they to us.'

'Had not Richard Fotheringay already come too close?' I said to Adam. 'Richard had copulated with Formosa, and caused violent orgasm in one of the undead. Come to that, all of you saw Formosa masturbating and heard her sing a song which suggested she was a dead woman pretending to be a live one. Surely all this was dangerously close?'

'Cinquemani assured us,' said Adam, 'that nothing which had happened so far, nothing, that is, which the members of the Order actually knew about, would cause them to "dispose" of us. Let us only have care for the future.'

'*Not* really a very helpful remark. The idea of that lot arriv-

ing for feasts of love or intellect at your Palazzo—so watch
your tongue and your prickle in case you go over the top, boys,
and get the chopper. It seems to me,' I said, 'that the only solution to your problem was an immediate posting out of Venice,
if possible right out of Italy. Let the brothers and sisters find
somebody else for Fellowship.'

'*Precisely*,' said Adam. 'But before we could get ourselves
posted, we had to get back to Venice, tidy up and hand over the
Pox Poopers' Department. And arrange to move it somewhere
else, so that our successors would not have demanding visitors
from Marciume or Tetro. We therefore drove back to Venice
very fast indeed—no Greek Temples at Pæstum on that trip
—to settle affairs at the Baldinucci and clear out of the place as
soon as possible.'

A few days later (Adam began to wind up his story) Adam,
Fotheringay and Jamieson had gathered for a farewell drink by
the little dell with the capering Satyr. All papers were boxed
and gone from the Palazzo Baldinucci; the flat was pristine;
their postings home to England had been arranged on compassionate grounds (the hand of Serjeant Jamieson had been swift
and deft); successors to their office had been found, and housed
at the other end of Venice; Adam and Co. themselves would
leave the garden and the Palazzo for ever as soon as they had
drunk their bottle.

'To that gay little Satyr,' Fotheringay proposed.

'Our Satyr,' said Jamieson.

'The spirit of summer,' said Adam.

'And to absent friends,' said Richard Fotheringay, lifting his
glass to the North East, in the direction of Marciume.

'Some of them still present,' said Colonnello Cinquemani's
voice from behind. 'Formosa and I thought you might like to
see us . . . since you are about to depart for good. The rest are
on their way back to Marciume; we two missed the boat, so to
speak.'

'There will be others?' Adam said.

'No doubt, for those that want them,' Cinquemani said. Holding Formosa's arm, he drew her round the end of the stone bench and on to the narrow margin between the bench and the edge of the dell.

'Formosa has a request,' said Cinquemani.

'Take me with you,' said Formosa: 'one of you, take me with you.'

'You are deserting your comrades?' said Richard Fotheringay.

'Your friendship means more to me than my comrades.'

'You hardly know us,' Adam said.

'You are the only friends I have apart from my colleagues. I have been with you on two occasions. That is enough. Your company—and the sight I had of the wide and beautiful world, the first for many years, on the way to and from Ustica—have made me long to leave Marciume and go with someone who will take me.'

'I am married with a son,' Serjeant Jamieson said.

'Ricardo?' said Formosa.

'I hope to become a scientist,' replied Richard; 'I have preparation to do, I have time lost in the war to make up. I cannot accommodate or care for a woman.'

'I should make no demands.'

'You could not help it.' Fotheringay was about to say more, but thought better of it and merely shook his head.

'Adam?'

'When I leave the Army, Formosa, I shall be a poor undergraduate with my way to make.'

'Undergraduate?'

'Student, if you like.'

'I could help you . . . in many ways.'

'I cannot get you back to England,' said Adam: 'it requires tickets, papers, permissions . . . that would be quite unobtainable as things are now.'

'But if you married me? The authorities would let me go with you. I could leave you when we get to England, as soon as you tired of me. At least I should have escaped into the world. You have no idea how horrible it will be for me if I return to Marcium . . .'

'But of course I had,' said Adam to me over the empty decanter. 'And she probably knew that I had, knew that Cinquemani had told us of the hideous labours and loneliness that stretched before her for ever. I could not leave her. I had no feelings of love for her, or even of liking or attraction; only pity, pity for a human being—though I knew very well she was not—whose sentence was fiendish and perpetual. I could not leave her. One at least from that accursed but blameless crew could be saved, in a fashion, and I must save her.

'She has done what she can in return. She has long since endeared herself to me, to the extent that I never wished her to leave me, as she once planned. She makes love, more fiercely yet more tenderly than any human being I have known. She is very strong, she works for me, she protects me, she never sleeps, except for a period, every two or three years, when I arrange, through Cinquemani, that she should retire briefly to the catacombs at Ustica, at a time when none of her brothers or sisters are there.'

'Do they know what became of her?'

'No. Cinquemani will never tell them—he swore. Even if they did know, they could not reach her without help he will not give them. Look, look over there. She must have come to take me home. She worries after me sometimes.'

A figure in a long black dress was now to be seen across the room, holding and leaning on Mr Symonds' chest-high lectern.

'Formosa . . .'

The figure slowly released the lectern and lurched forwards. Does she drink, I wondered? Adam looked puzzled. He rose, offered a hand to steady her.

'This is my friend, Simon Raven . . . Simon, my wife Formosa.'

I rose and we shook hands. Her Titian hair was brilliant,

even in the low light from the table-lamp. Her hand was limp and very wet. There was a faint, sweet smell coming from her, not altogether agreeable.

'I did not want to disturb you,' she said. 'But there is urgency, Adam. You must persuade Cinquemani to arrange for me to go to Ustica. At once.'

'But you have only just returned from Ustica.'

'I know. Something has gone wrong.'

Jamieson came in. He switched on the lights. He was wearing a dark grey suit with the Brigade tie.

'I have had a telephone call at my house, gentlemen, from Colonel Cinquemani. Good evening, Mrs Ogilvie,' Jamieson said to Formosa, who sagged into a chair and drooped over the table.

Jamieson moved very close to Adam. 'The disease of the lepers of Marciume,' he said, 'has proved resistant to the sedative drug they were given. It was likely to happen, sooner or later. It seems that the patients had been growing restless and disobedient for some time. So Thrasymedes made some alteration in the formula for the elixir, which he thought would strengthen it. But by some chemical quirk—or some error of Thrasymedes—it drove the lepers mad. They have attacked the brothers and sisters of the Order—raped them—torn them to pieces with their hands . . . thrown the shreds and gobbets into the Lagoon. We had better look to your wife.'

All three of us turned toward her; but the thing that had been Formosa was quivering and sinking. Her face was liquefying jelly, dripping, then descending with a kind of suck, on to the tablecloth.

'She had escaped the Order for a time,' said Jamieson, 'but not the bond. Their fate is her fate.'

'An—an ambulance?' croaked Adam.

'No, sir. It will be of no use at all. Liquids one can mop up, and clean away the stain. Pithy and colloidal substances we can dispose of. Our methods of dealing with the—superfluous— are modern and comprehensive.'

'But what shall I *say* when she is gone?'

'You have kept her very quiet, sir, all this time. Your guest here did not know until tonight. For the benefit of those few of your friends who might enquire ... the truth to Doctor Fotheringay, I think. Cinquemani will guess for himself. For any others, Mrs Ogilvie has had a nervous break-down and has gone into retreat abroad.'

'I shall of course hold my tongue,' I said.

'So I supposed, sir. But if you prefer,' said Jamieson to Adam, 'we could call the police. They know of spontaneous combustion. Why should there not be spontaneous decomposition?'

'No police,' said Adam. 'Disposal. What else ... in all the circumstances?'

'Just so, sir.'

'What,' I said, 'will they do with the lepers on Marciume?'

'That, sir, is somebody else's problem. I imagine that the final solution will now be applied, as it should have been a very long time ago.'

REMEMBER YOUR GRAMMAR

I was rather pleased when James Lauderdale turned up in Venice last month. Late November has never been a time when one's friends go there, least of all these days with so many of the hotels closed. So I was glad to see James's familiar face, and happy to have him with me on the walks we went. Often in November the weather in Venice is clear and blue, more beautiful than at any other season of the year; but even on the brightest of days, a sudden mist will creep down a passage from the *Laguna Morta*, making the best known campos murky and alien, distorting angles and falsifying distance, gathering round you in dumb hostility, compelling you to look behind for the man who is never there . . . and then, on one's walks, one is glad of company.

James Lauderdale was staying out on the Zattere, in a *pensione* which he swore Ruskin had patronised, but which I knew had not existed before 1920. Typical of James to be so inaccurate. A passionate amateur antiquarian, he had never yet got anything entirely right. His Norman doorways always turned out to be 19th century restorations, and clumsy ones at that; his gold was always silver-gilt. But his curiosity and exuberance made him tremendous fun to be with, particularly in a place like Venice; and every morning I would wait impatiently in my hotel by the Rialto bridge for James to come rattling over from the Zattere and cart me off on whatever expedition he fancied.

One day, the last day of November, he suggested a stroll up through the old Jewish quarter to the church of the Madonna dell'Orto. He wanted to see its cloister. As it happened, the cloister was closed (as it often is) and there was no one around to let us in; so since it was still too early for lunch, we loitered a bit on the way home. We took a different route from the one by which we had come. We walked along a *rio*, which came out into the larger canal of the Misericordia, and we stood on a bridge for a while: in front of us were the waters of the Misericordia, to our left the tiny campo of the Abbazia, to our right the huge building, like a kind of urban barn, that had once been the school of the Misericordia. And then I drew James's attention to something which I had often noticed before. In a small alcove, between the vast school and the *rio* above which we were standing, there was and is a patch of rough grass, much of which is covered with nettles and bramble. Among the nettles, if you look carefully, there are two or three square white stones, set there in the manner of tombstones in an overgrown cemetery, and yet unlike most tombstones for being too squat ... neither long and flat, as horizontal tombstones are, nor tall and thin like the vertical ones.

'I've often wondered about these stones,' I said. 'Odd, a little wilderness like that in the middle of Venice.'

As I might have known, James Lauderdale had an instant and romantic theory to propound.

'Private graveyard,' he said. 'Used by the School in the old days to dispose of unwanted bodies, suicides and so on.'

'The stones don't look right,' I told him. 'Anyway, suicides and so on shouldn't have had stones at all. They should just have been put away out of sight.'

'Then perhaps it was a regular cemetery. Perhaps it was pukka hallowed ground which the School had permission to use. In any case, it's certainly an oddity, as you say, and it requires investigation.'

'How are you going to get into it?' I said.

I should explain that the alcove was between two massive buttresses that projected from the east end of the School right down to the edge of the *rio*. There was thus no way into it from the bridge on which we stood, or from the Fondamenta, the large quayside, which marched along the south wall of the Misericordia, between it and its eponymous canal.

'By boat?' said James.

But the level of the *rio*, I pointed out, was too low. There was a good nine feet of slimy stone between the surface of the water and the grass verge of the alcove above it. There were no steps; and no one could possibly have clambered up from a boat.

'Then there must be a way through the School itself. There must be a door out of this end of the School and into that little wilderness. There's something which might answer half-hidden in that angle there. We'll go into the School now,' he said, with his usual immediacy, 'and inquire.' The entrance to the School, which these days is used as a youth centre, is at the west end, i.e., at the opposite end from where we now were. We walked off the bridge, along the Fondamenta, eventually found a large door and in it a janitor who was about to lock it up. James bombarded him with enthusiastic and vile Italian.

No, said the janitor when he was allowed to speak, he could not show the *signori* the way to the garden (for that was what he called it). To start with, it was time he went home for his *pranzo*; secondly, the door was a special door and only the director of the centre had a key. Ah, said James Lauderdale; could we come back and see the director later? Had we not noticed, said the janitor, that the day was Sunday? The centre was closed on Sunday from noon onwards, and all of Monday, too, of course. If we came back on Tuesday . . .

'Garden?' said James as we went on our way towards our own lunch. 'Why should he call it that?'

I pictured in my mind the square stones among the nettles. I remembered the bare brambles and the long, damp grass. I thought of those nine feet of slimy stone plummeting down from the verge of the grass to the surface of the *rio* below, and of the massive buttresses which guarded the alcove on either side.

'Why should he call it a garden?' James repeated.

'Euphemism,' I said. 'In Latin countries you call unpleasant things by a polite name in case the wrong person is listening. I'm glad, now I come to think of it, that we can't get in.'

'We can—on Tuesday.'

But as you shall hear, we got in sooner than that.

That evening, we went to the winter casino in the Palazzo Vendramin. Casinos do not close on Sundays in Italy, whatever youth centres may or may not do; they simply increase the stakes. James had an infallible system of play, which cleaned him out of all the cash he was carrying with remorseless brevity. Much the same happened to me. And so, when we had perforce finished our gaming, it was still too early to go straight home.

'We'll walk a long way round,' James said. 'Up to the lagoon and back by Zanipolo. Do us good after this frowsty hole.'

'There's a heavy mist,' I said. 'Let's stick to the main streets and have a few drinks *en route*.'

'Never mind your dipsomania, Simon. We need exercise.'

So we went a long way round. But the mist, swirling over us at some vital junction, must have tricked us. For, suddenly, we emerged from a passage, not into a cross passage as we should have, but onto a quayside along a broad canal. The canal of the Misericordia. We were approaching the west end of the School. The door was open and there were lights inside.

'Open,' said James.

'That janitor said it was closed after midday on Sundays.'

'You can see for yourself.'

We stepped in out of the fog, some of which was hanging about in the small atrium which we found we had entered. At first, it was difficult to see; then I distinguished a desk, and, sitting behind it, a small, lean man who was wearing a black beret. James at once started banging on about the wilderness over the *rio*.

'The garden,' said the man. 'You wish to go there?'

'Yes,' said the unstoppable James.

'Now?' said the man indifferently.

'Why not?'

'Why not indeed? You will need the key and a torch.' He handed both to James.

'Which way?'

'Through the gymnasium and into the changing-room. There's a low door next to the WC.'

Without rising, the man in the beret waved towards a curtained archway in the wall to our right. We went through the curtain and into the gymnasium. This was more brightly lit than the atrium, but not brilliantly; a few youths were playing ping-pong or billiards; they made none of the raucous and quarrelsome babble typical of Italians who are engaged in such pursuits; indeed, they were silent, except for a low and general murmur among them, and ignored us totally. We passed into the changing-room, found the low door, unlocked it without any trouble, and came out into the alcove which one of the buttresses made with the main building. The fog concealed the bridge on which we had stood that morning, but was not at all thick over our patch of grass.

At once, James Lauderdale took the torch to the most prominent of the square stones among the nettles. I stood apart. I had not wished to come, I had been sucked in, so to say, in the wake of James's enthusiasm—which would soon, I hoped, exhaust itself and let us both leave.

'An inscription,' called James.

Hell, I thought; that will delay us.

'Bloody nettles,' James said. 'What one goes through in the cause of knowledge.' Then 'AUGUSTUS LARI,' he spelt out. 'Ouch, bloody nettles. *Sepultus hic Kal Dec MDCCXXV.* "Buried here on the Kalends of December, i.e. the first of December 1725." There's something more.'

Hell; more delay.

'An epitaph,' called James. '*Qui novit semper noluit.* "Anyone who knew him always wished he didn't." Witty Latin but not very charitable. And more of it: *Noli novisse.* "Do not wish to have known him"—that is, "Be glad you didn't," I suppose. And I think there's even more underneath. Funny I didn't spot it at first.'

A puff of wind scattered the fog; briefly I saw the *rio* below and the bridge over it; then the fog re-formed, blotting out the bridge and the *rio* but staying almost clear of the wilderness. Cut off, I thought; cut off on this little patch.

'Come on, James. I'm cold. Time to go.'

'I tell you there's something else carved here. In smaller letters, down near the grass.'

'*For Christ's sake!* We can come back again when it's light.'

I almost ran through the gymnasium. The sullen boys still murmured over their games. James caught me up by the desk in the atrium.

'Can we come tomorrow?' he said to the man in the black beret.

'Tomorrow they're closed,' I said.

'Monday.'

'You can come,' said the man, half ignoring, half answering my objection. 'Come early, and the door will be opened to you.'

As we left the School, the fog lifted. We made our way without difficulty towards the Rialto bridge.

'Lucky they were open after all,' said James.

'It's all wrong,' I said, remembering something.

'What is?'

'*Sepultus hic* on that stone. "Buried here" . . . *with the date*. It shouldn't give the date of the burial but that of the death. It should have said *obiit* or *mortuus* . . . one of the words meaning "died." '

'Don't be so pedantic. Perhaps Signor Augustus Lari was buried the same day he died. That would support my theory about the place being used for suicides.'

'There is another possibility.'

'Not that I can see. Do you want to come with me tomorrow morning?'

'No,' I said.

'Very nervy all of a sudden. Just because of *sepultus hic?*'

'There's something else wrong with that inscription. I can't place it yet, but there is.'

We came to the Rialto bridge. James crossed it, on his way to the Zattere. I went to my own hotel. We had agreed that he would call for me there the next morning, as soon as he had finished his early visit to the garden of the Misericordia.

That night I dreamed continuously. I was thirteen again, doing my scholarship examinations. Latin. Long proses, some verses, some unseens. Every now and then I woke, when I slept again I was still in the examination room. Greek now. Mathematics. Then Latin once more. Grammar. Question: What is a Defective Verb? Answer ... answer ... but no answer would come—until I woke once more, remembering it. A Defective Verb is a verb which lacks one or more tenses and uses others to replace them. Classic instance: *noscere*, to know. Which never uses the present tense, but substitutes its perfect or aorist *novi* (which should mean 'I have known' or 'I knew') to express the present 'I know'. *Qui novit semper noluit*, that stone had written on it. 'Whoever knew him always wished he didn't.' James had translated: an unkind epitaph. But it did not mean that. *Novit* stood for the present tense and *voluit*, by the rules of sequence, must be perfect and not aorist. Thus: 'Whoever *knows* him *has* always wished not to.' And *noli novisse*: not 'Do not wish to have known him,' i.e., 'Be glad you didn't,' as James had rendered; but simply, since *novisse* stood for the present infinitive, 'Do not wish to know him.' i.e. 'Shun him.' Not an epitaph, then: a warning. Spelt out: Do not wish to know him, because he is someone or something which those who know him have always wished they would never know. And what would that be? The nursery terror, I thought confusedly as I huddled on my clothes, the creature of the night which one has always suspected of existing and has always wished never to know for certain, never to meet face to face.

It was half past eight. 'Come early,' the man in the beret had said. I must hurry to James's *pensione*, to prevent him. But he was not there. He had gone out very early, the porter said. By the quay in front of the *pensione* I found a water taxi. To the School of the Misericordia. The door was closed, I rang the bell, the janitor of yesterday appeared. No. He had not seen James.

'I told you yesterday,' he said, 'the centre is closed on Sundays from noon and all of Monday. Which is today. I have just arrived and no one is here but me.'

Disregarding his protest, I ran through the atrium, through the gymnasium, through the changing-room to the little door by the WC. The key was in it. (Had James left it there? Who had let him into the building?) I stepped out into the enclave. Nobody. That stone square James had examined—the nettles had been trampled for some distance around it. By James last night, of course. No; *newly* trampled. By James this morning? Then where was he? I looked at the stone itself. There was the epitaph, which he had read to me. And there, in smaller letters, down near the grass, was the further inscription which I had not let him stay to read.

JACOBUS LAUDERDALE
Sepultus hic Kal. Dec. MCMLXXV

'James Lauderdale, buried here on December the first 1975.' But that's today, I thought, this very morning.

'James,' I called stupidly. 'Oh, James.'

And had no answer.

THE TEAM PHOTOGRAPH

The photograph of the school First XI taken at the end of July 1945 was not of eleven boys but of twelve. This was because Otho de Freville, the head of the school, had bullied Frank Rawlings, captain of cricket, into awarding a twelfth cap, which went to Otho himself. This honour Otho had done nothing to deserve except to play as a substitute against Eton, which is to say that he fielded (in a fashion) for about 32 minutes before the match was murdered just after noon, by rain.

That was in June. Weeks later, a day or two before 'Colour Sunday' (when the caps for all the XIs were finally made up and announced), Otho said to Frank Rawlings, 'A fellow who was chosen to take the field against Eton deserves his First XI cap.'

'It was your only match,' said Frank Rawlings, 'and you weren't chosen. You were a substitute for Daniel Spinoza, who unfortunately had to be away.'

And even that, as Frank remarked to me later when reporting the conversation, was a euphemistic statement of the affair. In fact, Otho had gone round and about, some days before the Eton match, telling everyone that Spinoza looked too 'foreign' to be allowed to represent the school against Eton. It would be all right in most other matches, Otho conceded—against Westminster or Harrow, if not, perhaps, against Winchester; but most definitely not in the match against Eton. Yes, yes, Otho quite understood that Spinoza was our only left-arm spin-bowler and was also a useful batsman at number seven or eight (provided the opposition's fast men had been taken off); but when it came to the fixture against Eton such considerations must give way to those of social propriety. It simply was not proper to allow someone as . . . er . . . *swarthy* as Spinoza to turn out on this occasion.

For a time Frank Rawlings deprecated this disgraceful sentiment; but Daniel Spinoza himself, a retiring and scholarly boy, had been so disturbed by all the talk that he eventually told Frank that he would, in any case, be away during the Eton match for an interview with an Appointments Board, though everyone knew very well (because others were to attend it) that the Board did not commence until the afternoon of the day after the match and that Spinoza could easily have made the journey to London that morning. All of us, however, whether in the XI or not, maintained a discreet (or shifty) silence in the matter; and so Otho played instead, or at least sauntered about on the field in his beautifully pressed and laundered kit, until the rains came.

In subsequent matches, Spinoza resumed his place; he finished the season with a bowling average of 9.3 (20 wickets at a cost of 186) and a batting average of 16.6 recurring (highest score 41 not out), and had indeed received his cap in mid-June, not long after the infamous Eton affair. Spinoza's cap was the ninth of the XI; the tenth and eleventh were awarded in early July; and all eleven capped players warned to appear at three of the afternoon on 'Colour (or Capping) Sunday' for the First XI photograph.

'Give twelve caps and give me the twelfth,' Otho had said to Frank Rawlings on the Thursday before. 'I want to be in that photo on Sunday. It will make a fitting end to my career in this place.'

'I can only award eleven caps,' Frank Rawlings said, 'and I have already done so.'

'You are captain of cricket and you can do what you wish. Even the Head Man cannot interfere. If anyone makes a row, you can always say that I did, when all is said, play against Eton.'

Et cetera. Et cetera. Frank Rawlings was a tired man (after the whole season, after gruelling exams) and he wanted peace. Otho was a persistent man who could and would, at a need, make trouble. It was time for all to part, thought Frank, without discordance; the whole thing would in any case be forgotten by the following September, when men's minds turned to football and he himself would be far away (albeit the war in Europe was now over) serving his king.

So Frank agreed. Otho was posted on the early morning of 'Colour Sunday' (the last of the school year) as being the twelfth of the First XI caps. That afternoon, when the photograph was taken in front of the pavilion, five men sat for it in the front row as usual, and seven stood behind them instead of six.

Spinoza arrived late and hustled into the standing line of seven just inside Otho, although he should, such was his seniority, have been standing in the middle of the row and not next to Otho, who as last cap of all was at the end of it.

'Just a minute,' said Otho to the photographer. 'This boy on my left should be much further in. I don't want him anywhere near me.'

'Does it matter?' said the photographer. 'I believe there is a world war on, or was until the other day. Although it is a Sunday, I have more important things to do than humour the fads of pampered boys.'

(The 'post-war spirit', you see, was catching on fast.)

Now, Spinoza could well have moved into his right place while the photographer was asserting himself with this speech, but apparently he chose not to; and so the photograph was taken with Otho outside Spinoza on the left (as you looked at it) of the back row. Then the First XI of 1945 shook hands, with just a tear or two, and went on their ways . . . all except for Daniel Spinoza, who did indeed go on his way, but shed no tear and shook no hand.

And now it is 1985, forty years on (as the song has it), and Otho de Freville is dead. Since he made quite a mark as a publisher of technical books, his obituary in *The Daily Telegraph* (on a thin day for deaths) is prominent. There is also a picture, in which Otho looks a bit flea-bitten. So I have hunted out my copy of the First XI photograph of 1945 in order to remind myself, out of interest rather than affection, what Otho had looked like on the verge of his spunky youth.

He isn't there. Spinoza is there, but now he is at the end of the back row of six boys only.

How very peculiar. I am sure I have remembered correctly all the things I have just been telling you. Otho *must* be there; only he isn't. I do hope my memory hasn't collapsed. I could have sworn, even after forty years . . . No good worrying. Next week I shall be seeing Frank Rawlings at Lord's Test. I shall ask him if he remembers what I remember, and if so, whether he can explain the thing.

'Well, now,' said Frank Rawlings this afternoon at Lord's. 'For a start, *I* haven't got a copy of that photo. My wife Lileth threw it away. She is jealous of my past, which of course includes you: so I told her the firm was sending me to Birmingham for the day. I only hope she doesn't see me sitting here on television. Where was I?'

'Our old team photograph.'

'Oh, yes. Several times over the years, however, I have seen a copy of it in magazines or newspapers. After all, it includes an England cricketer, a judge of appeal, and about the only politician of probity the country has had for thirty years. So one sees it from time to time in the public prints. Always, as far as I recall, it has shown Otho de Freville and Daniel Spinoza standing together at the end of the back row, Spinoza being inside Otho.'

'Just as I remember from the day it was taken,' I said.

'But now you say that your copy no longer includes Otho?'

'Gone. Clean gone.'

A grey, stooping, seedily dressed man worked his way along our row and inserted himself on the bench in the yard or so we had left between us for comfort.

'Steady on, sir,' I said. 'There's not room for the three of us.'

'Enough,' he said, 'for an old companion. Daniel Spinoza.'

'Spinoza?' said Frank. 'I haven't seen you since—'

'Since 1945,' said the newcomer. 'Nor has Raven here. I have been in another country. In the East . . . whence my family came. I hated this country . . . where people said things about me such as de Freville once said. And no one, not one of you in the XI, stood up for me. I hated you all, more and more over the years, when I took out that photograph to look at you . . . in another country, in the East. Yes, I hated you all; but I hated de Freville the most.'

'And yet,' I said, 'you stood next to him in the photograph. You needn't have done, you shouldn't have done, but you did.'

'I had my reasons. Proximity among them.' He was, I reflected, tiresomely proximate to Frank and myself now. 'Of course, we were young then,' he went on, 'and there was no hurry. After forty years time is running short. Things are changing fast, now that I am back again from that other country in the East. Go home, Raven: go home and look at that photograph.'

'I have,' I said.

'Go home and look again. Why didn't you stand up for me, for your companion? None of you did,' he muttered, and began to rise.

'I stood up for you,' said Frank.

'Yes. A little. Not for long. You breathed the same sigh of relief as the rest of them when I made my excuse. I remembered that, all those hours in the East I spent looking at that photograph of my companions. But you were the best of them. Not like de Freville with his malice, or Raven here, with his indifference.'

He began to shamble away along the row. Then he looked back.

'Go home and look again,' he called in a high voice, 'at the XI of 1945.'

So now I am looking again.

Spinoza is grinning. Next to him, where Otho de Freville once was and then was not, a kind of waxwork is standing, of a figure wearing beautifully pressed white flannel trousers and a fine silk shirt, both of a quality so difficult to obtain during the war, and both now stained by some sort of oozing flux.

I myself am sitting where I sat on that July afternoon, at the end of the first row, just in front of the grinning Spinoza. I, too, am grinning, but not in the same manner as Spinoza. As I look at myself in the photograph, I am fascinated by the tufts and blotches on my slimy pate where, surely, forty years ago, there had been bright auburn waves ... where, even now, there is a healthy brown growth. Or is there? Very soon I must go and look into the glass.

THE SARCOPHAGUS

'Whatever happens,' said Julian, 'we must not get trapped in some restaurant by the French Sunday *déjeuner*.'

'We must eat,' said Marigold.

'Certainly. And we must take not more than half an hour in so doing. Since we cut Mass this morning in order to save time, we cannot, in decency, linger over luncheon.'

'I still don't see what the hurry is.'

'We have a schedule. You know that. I'm sure we can find a snack bar somewhere.'

'It's now a quarter past one,' said Marigold, 'and we are just ten miles short of Cahors. Although Cahors is not the sort of place to have a snack bar, it may well have a brasserie.'

'On Sundays,' said Julian, 'brasseries are every bit as bad as fully-fledged restaurants. They withdraw the *carte* and all the shorter menus, and you wind up taking three hours, and paying a hundred francs a head for the privilege of sitting in a mass of yowling infants and smelly old women.'

'The nearest place which is touristy enough to have a snack bar is Albi.'

'Albi is not on our route. We are going through Caussade, Montauban, Toulouse and Carcassone, and thence on to the autoroute. Caussade and Montauban are pretty old-fashioned, but there might well be a snack bar in Toulouse.'

'Julian dear. It is twenty past one. I cannot wait for my lunch until we reach Toulouse. We must eat in Cahors. Please, darling: after all, it is my birthday.'

'Well, I suppose it is,' said Julian in a tone of strictly limited concession. 'So, if you really want to, we can eat in Cahors. So long as we don't take more than forty minutes at the outside.'

'But sweetheart: what *is* the hurry?'

'You know very well what the hurry is.'

'You think the hotel will let the rooms go?'

'No Marigold. The hotel will not let the rooms go. The agency has paid in advance and warned the management that we may be late.'

'Then you're worried lest we may be too late for dinner.'

'No, Marigold. It would not worry me in the least if, just for once, we had no dinner.'

'No dinner . . . on my birthday?'

'It would not, I say, worry me. But dinner there will assuredly be, either *en route*, or, more probably, when we reach the hotel . . . which, as you well know, is an extremely expensive hotel and provides delicious food for twenty-four hours in twenty-four. If one is too late to dine in the public rooms, one will be served, with only slightly less elaboration, in one's own suite.'

'All right. You're not afraid of the rooms being given away and you're not afraid of missing dinner. So what the hell is the hurry?'

'I have explained often enough. You really should have understood by now.'

'No, Julian. You have not explained. All you have said is that we must be in Arles before eight o'clock.'

'That is correct, Marigold. We must be in Arles—in the right place in Arles—by eight p.m., and this means entering Arles not later than 7.40 p.m., to be on the safe side.'

'It'll take no time at all once we're on the autoroute.'

'We're still a very long way from being on the autoroute. And don't forget: we'll have to come off it in order to enter Arles.'

'*That* won't take long.'

'It might, with the Sunday traffic. All the cits and proles going home.'

'You can't expect . . . even at your age . . . to have the roads all to yourself.'

'Indeed I don't. That is why I insist that luncheon should take a maximum of forty minutes.'

'Here we are in Cahors now . . . no snack bar that I can see
. . . there's a brasserie . . . but it's shut. *I* know, sweetheart, just
the very thing. The red Michelin says that there's a swish hotel
just outside Cahors at a place called Mercues. It's not as swish
as where we're going tonight, but it's quite swish enough to
understand about us being in a hurry and to let us have just one
thing off the *carte* instead of a full lunch. Fresh *foie gras*, perhaps.
I've always wanted to try that, although they're so beastly to
the poor geese, and the Michelin says it's one of their speciali-
ties.'

'You just *could* be right, Marigold. How many towers does
Michelin award the hotel?'

'Three towers in red. And two rosettes for its food.'

'Three towers in red. Yes. That should make it—er—"swish"
enough to be obliging to people like us . . .'

★   ★   ★

'The worst of both worlds,' Julian said.

'The fresh *foie gras* was delicious.'

'It was listed at eighty francs a cover. But they charged the
minimum Sunday menu charge of one hundred and seventy
francs a head *and* they took for ever to serve us.'

'They were very busy.'

'That's why I wanted to go to a snack bar.'

'There weren't any.' Marigold said. 'Anyhow, there's oodles
of time. According to the map we are now less than 250 kilometres from Narbonne, where we get on to the autoroute. If
we manage that by about six p.m. . . .'

'. . . If,' snapped Julian. 'It's now after three, thanks to your
swish hotel.'

'You should be able to average eighty kilometres an hour on
a road like this . . . with a perfectly marvellous car like this. And
once on the autoroute you'll have two hours to do the two hundred kilometres to Arles and get to where you want to be inside
it. With this lovely drag it's just child's play.'

'Suppose some of the autoroute is up for repair? Damnation. A bicycling race. Get out of my way, you frightful frog.'

'Julian darling, for Christ's sake. Can't you see that man holding up his hand? I think he's some kind of marshal.'

'They've no right to impede the traffic.'

'You know very well they always have bicycle races on Sundays. If it's so important that we get to Arles by eight, why, for God's sake, Julian, did we not come further south yesterday. If we'd tried at all, yesterday, we could have been within easy distance of Arles . . . Mass or no Mass, Sunday lunch or no Sunday lunch, cyclists or no fucking cyclists.'

'You know I hate your using that word. And you know very well why we didn't come further south yesterday. I explained often enough.'

'You explained nothing. You just stated that we had to spend the night at Poitiers.'

'Yes. The hotel had been booked by the agency.'

'But Julian. It isn't actually a crime to pass up a hotel booking. I bet the agency had already paid.'

'That is correct.'

'Then we could have driven on with clear consciences, knowing that we hadn't let the hotel down, at least as far as Brive-la-Gaillarde.'

'No, we couldn't have. Rooms were booked and paid for in Poitiers.'

'Booked and paid for . . . Julian, angel, you don't mean you were thinking of the money?'

'Of course not.'

'I mean, you were a bit funny just now about the price of lunch.'

'That was different. That was a deliberate swindle; they were screwing us to pieces, Marigold, because they knew that on Sunday we had no option. That I object to; but I wouldn't in the least have minded spending money on rooms I didn't use in Poitiers, because in that case I should have been acting of my own free will and choice.'

'Then why didn't you act of your own free will and choice, and drive us on to Brive-la-Gaillarde? Then there would not have been this ridiculous panic now.'

'Thank God, that frog is letting us go. Mercy mon sewer . . . Marigold, we *had* to spend the night in Poitiers, just as we *have* to be in a certain place in Arles by eight p.m., and then *have* to go to the hotel into which we are booked at Les Baux.'

'Hmmm, Julian, did you know that the heir to the Principality of Monaco is called the Marquis des Baux?'

'No I didn't.'

'Lots of people think he's called the Duke of Monte Carlo. But he isn't. He's called the Marquis des Baux, one of the family titles. At one period the Princes of Monaco had lordships and baronies all over France, several counties and viscounties.'

'. . . Viscount-*cies* . . .'

'. . . And also a duchy or two, but the only marquisate they had was this Marquisate of Les Baux. That made it special, so I suppose that's why the heir to the Principality of Monaco chose to be called the Mar . . .'

'. . . Marigold. Are you setting up as a lecturer in heraldry? What in heaven's name has all this to do with us?'

'I thought you might be interested, sweetie. You're such a colossal snob. Anyway, it *does* have to do with us, because it has to do with Les Baux, and that (if heaven permits) is where we are to lay our heads this night.'

'It is hardly relevant to our purpose in going there.'

'Julian, Julian: just what *is* our bloody purpose in going there?'

'You know I hate that word on your lips. Any of those words. Our purpose in going to Les Baux is the same as our purpose in spending last night in Poitiers and in reaching Arles by eight this evening. Hell and death. More of those infernal bicyclists.'

'We're not getting on too badly, even so. And I think Julian, to judge from the map, that some of the road between Toulouse and Narbonne is now dual carriageway. We'll make it, don't you worry.'

'We need petrol. Within . . . thirty miles.'

'There'll be somewhere. Tell me Julian, sweetie-pie: what would happen if we *didn't* arrive in Arles before eight?'

'Nothing. That's the trouble. Something had to happen . . . and did happen . . . at Poitiers; something must now happen at Arles; and then something must happen at Les Baux. If we are late in Arles, nothing can happen there, the sequence will then have been interrupted, nothing will happen at Les Baux either, and my whole effort will have been wasted.'

'Am I anything to do with these happenings?'

'You are a necessary condition of their occurrence.'

'I didn't notice anything last night.'

'You wouldn't have. You were asleep.'

'Shall I notice anything at Arles? They're waving you on, darling.'

'I hope that's the last of these races.'

'Shall I notice anything at Arles, Julian?'

'I doubt it. You just have to be there. An open garage. You never know on Sunday . . . we may as well fill up while we can.'

★   ★   ★

'There's the entrance to the autoroute,' said Marigold. 'Just before six. We're going to skate it. Does it matter what time we get to Les Baux?'

'Not really . . . provided it's before midnight. There should be no problem about that. It's barely half an hour from Arles.'

'How long shall we be at Arles?'

'Not long. We have to be down in the Alyscamps by eight. Something will happen there . . . before 8.30.'

'The Alyscamps, Julian?'

'Yes, you know. The place where all those Roman sarcophagi are. Along the avenue, under the trees.'

'I've never been there.' She took a green Michelin from the glove compartment and flicked through the pages. 'Once a pagan burial ground,' she announced, 'but a Christian cemetery later. Legend says that Roland was miraculously brought to Arles and buried there. The whole place was cut up by the railway and now there's only one avenue left, with a ruined church, Saint Honorat, at the end of it. It also says that in more recent times the sarcophagi have been so much prized that they've often been given to distinguished guests as presents. What a funny sort of present.'

'They're very decorative.'

'Stone coffins,' she said. 'Ugh. Anyway, why the Alyscamps?'

'That's where I was told.'

Marigold looked down at the Michelin.

'The French have fenced the place in,' she said, 'and charge two francs for admission. The gates will be closed by the time we get there.'

'Not to us. Not on Sunday . . . not if we're there by eight.'

'How very peculiar you're being. You never mentioned any of this before we left England.'

'Would you have come if I had?'

'Of course. None of it matters to me,' said Marigold.

'Oh doesn't it?'

'Why should it?'

'Because, as I told you, you are the necessary condition of it.'

'For Christ's sake, Julian. Stop being all knowing and mysterious, and tell me what's going on.'

'You'll find out at the Alyscamps.'

'You said I wouldn't notice anything.'

'You'll find out what's going on, all the same.'

'I don't understand.'

'Just wait and see, like a good girl.'

'Stop talking to me as if I were a baby. I'm sixteen today. A grown woman.'

'Very well. Behave like one. Stop yattering away like a nine-year-old, and pass me a fruit pastille from that tube in the glove compartment.'

*   *   *

'Mister Julian Leigh,' said the receptionist at Les Baux; then, with an oily smirk, 'and his daughter, Miss Marigold Leigh. I shall require your passport, sir, under existing regulations, but not Miss Marigold's. He consulted a large book. 'A suite for you, Mr Leigh ... and a large bedroom, with private bath of course, for the young lady. All in order. The basic charge has already been paid by the World Travellers' Agency, whom we are to invoke for payment of any additional charges. Most satisfactory. Now come this way, if you please ... If you care to be ready within half an hour, you may dine downstairs; otherwise you will be very well attended to by the floor waiter ... though not quite *all* our dishes are available from room service. Your room, Miss Leigh ... and your apartments, Mr Leigh. Your luggage, as you see, is already up here.'

'Dinner upstairs or down, chuck?' Julian said.

'No dinner.'

'What's happened to that famous appetite? They have some of the most distinguished food in the world here.'

'I'm not hungry, I tell you. You said I'd notice nothing at the Alyscamps but that I'd find out what was going on. Well I noticed nothing and I found out nothing.'

'I wasn't, perhaps, strictly accurate. I should have said that you'd find out at the Alyscamps or a little while after. You're finding out now.'

'Nothing. I'm finding out nothing,' said Marigold. 'I only know that the idea of food disgusts me, and I feel horribly tired.'

'You've had a long day. A long last twenty-four hours, in fact. Let's think, let's remember. This time yesterday we were in Poitiers, and you were going to bed ... early, because we had an early start to make in the morning. Two hours later, just after midnight, very early this morning ... Sunday morning ... you became sixteen years old. That was the first thing that had to happen.'

'Why did it have to happen in Poitiers?'

'Because Poitiers was and is closely associated with Saint

Radegunde, a celibate of very firm, indeed forceful, personality. That you should become sixteen in Poitiers guaranteed, so to speak, the strength of your maidenhood on a birthday crucial in such matters.'

'Who wanted to do that?'

'I did. I sought instruction, and this, they said, was the way to do it. The combination of your sixteenth birthday, and the saintly Radegunde, *and* Sunday, would be, they said, a very potent influence.'

'They? I don't begin to understand what you're talking about.'

'You will. Let us continue our account of the last twenty-four hours. Despite a series of setbacks we arrived in Arles in time to reach the Alyscamps just before eight. At dusk. At dusk on Sundays in the Alyscamps they conduct a special private Mass in Saint Honorat, for although the church is ruined a side-chapel is still consecrated. And so we were admitted, on producing invitations to attend this private Mass . . .'

'. . . Who gave you the invitations?' Marigold said.

'They did. And so we were admitted, and we attended the Mass, which is sung in intercession for the souls of all the dead, whether pagan or Christian, who ever lay in the sarcophagi in the Alyscamps. A richly poetic notion. But this time there was an addition. *Your* soul was commended to God's mercy along with the rest.'

Marigold shuddered.

'I didn't hear my name,' she said.

'It was latinised and garbled. So of course, since you weren't expecting it, you didn't hear it. But *I* heard it. *They* had arranged for it to be included.'

'They?'

'And since you yourself were present, and since you are a believing Roman Catholic, and since you joined in the service in a spirit of assent, it follows that you too commended your soul to God's mercy . . .'

'. . . It's a trick . . .'

'. . . *That you commended your own soul*, in the same terms as the others were commended, that is, as the soul of one long dead who had lain in the Alyscamps. You didn't notice anything at the time; but as I told you you would, you soon began to find out what was going on. You have no appetite, Marigold; worse, the thought of food revolts you; and you are . . . "horribly tired." Sunday . . . your Sunday . . . the Sunday of your womanhood and your purification . . . of your intercession for yourself and of your salvation . . . is nearly done. There is only one other condition which we still have to observe. Ideally you should lie in a sarcophagus in the Alyscamps. But since this cannot be, you must at least lie in a sarcophagus which was once in the Alyscamps . . . and one such there is close at hand, which was procured from the Alyscamps to decorate the grounds of this hotel when it was still a chateau in the seventeenth century.'

'Why? Julian, why?'

'Why? That you may be a virgin going to your salvation. Dedicated to God before it is too late. A pert, forward, fleshy minx . . . for ever flirting with her own father, calling him darling, sweetie-pie, at the best, Julian . . . ?'

'. . . You told me to call you Julian.'

'. . . Today turned sixteen and reaching the age of nubility and consent . . . the soul of such a one is surely damned, unless it be purified at once and sent to God. *They* were clear enough about that.'

'THEY?'

'The nuns at your school, your convent. "Save Marigold from the world," they told me; "we will show you how. We will show you how to cast the spell . . . a holy spell. First, let her complete her sixteenth year and come to womanhood in the shadow of a saint of great and renowned chastity. And then . . ." No matter. The rest you have just heard from me.'

'They once asked me . . . did I not think I had a vocation to come among them? I said "no" and they were angry. This is their revenge.'

'They wanted you for God, not for themselves. As I do.'

Julian looked at his watch.

'Before midnight, they said. It is time for the sarcophagus, little Marigold. I have a knife here to make it quick and kind, in case the spell is slow or has somehow failed in strength.'

'But . . . but they'll know when they find me. They'll know that you . . .'

'No. They'll think it was some crude shepherd from these hills. Who found you, raped you, cut your throat . . . and thrust you into that sarcophagus.'

'Raped me? You're going to rape me first . . .'

'. . . To possess you. What matter? You are already purified and given to God. Since I am to save you, I shall first enjoy you. I alone. They said that God would understand.'

Marigold shrank away.

'You're raving bloody fucking bonkers,' she said.

'For heaven's sake, Marigold,' said Julian crossly. 'It was all agreed. I did tell you in London that it would be no good at all unless you said the words exactly right, particularly as we drew near the end. You know you're never meant to say "bloody" or "fucking," and as for "bonkers," words fail me. You were meant to say, "You must be insane . . . or utterly evil." Now you've spoilt it all and we shall have to go through the whole business all over again in order to recreate the illusion . . . my wonderful *ruined* Gothic illusion.'

'I'm sorry,' said Marigold. 'Somehow my concentration snapped. Not having dinner, that was it. Having to pretend I didn't want it because of that spell. Perhaps next time you could allow dinner in the routine. After all, healthy, hungry girls . . .'

'. . . It's really too bad of you. This is the only way that I can . . . that I can . . . er . . . manage, and now it's going to take me weeks to make all the right arrangements again. I've got to set up all those difficult Sunday bookings, and engage the monks to come to Saint Honorat's, and hire the cyclists to delay us . . . It will cost me a huge amount of money . . . all of which they insist on having in advance.'

'What can you expect,' said Marigold, 'with this sort of

circus? You should count your blessings. A few years ago we'd both have had to show our passports . . . and God knows what it would have cost you, getting me a fake one as your daughter.'

'That wouldn't have mattered. They know perfectly well you're not. They've seen dozens of my "daughters" during the last twenty years, and they've gone along with the pretence to please me . . . for a price, of course. But what annoys me is that they'll demand *another* great fat bribe for letting us do it in the sarcophagus in the garden next time, even though we haven't used it this.'

'You know,' said Marigold. 'I think you *are* getting mean about money, whatever you may say. So just think of all you'd have saved, if only you'd allowed me to have dinner.'

THE BOTTLE OF 1912

In the Spring of 1947 I returned, you might say, from the dead. Never mind what I had been doing. I suppose you would call me a spy; I had penetrated into a world so remote that it was a long time before I learned of the end of the war, and even longer before my task was done and I could make my way back, by slow and careful stages, to the Headquarters in Delhi. Here they were in the fever which precedes departure, for India would be independent in a few months; and besides being thus preoccupied, they were rather embarrassed to see me.

'We didn't expect to see *you* again,' said Stetson accusingly; 'we gave *you* up last summer.'

'It all took longer than we thought.'

'Evidently. How long will it take you to make out your report?'

'A week . . . ten days. And then I suppose I can go home?'

'Yes,' said Stetson, 'you can go home.'

'By the way,' I said, 'you should have all my mail here. I gave this as my holding address.'

'We did have it. But we sent it off to your next of kin when we ceased to expect you back. A married sister in Kent, I think?'

'That's right.'

'You'll just have to wait a few days longer for your bills. After all, you've waited some years already . . .'

Yes, I thought: four years. Ever since 1943 when I left England, reported to Stetson, and went off into the hills. A few days more would hardly matter. But I should like to have read those letters from my sister; to have heard the news of her husband and my little nephew and the farm in Kent. And there was another thing—something that had not really occurred to me in the mountains but was obvious now that I was back in the familiar world: my sister would think I was dead. Or at best missing. In 1946 she would have received the parcel with my mail in it, along with a polite letter from Stetson '... Very much regret ... has failed to report back ... must reluctantly conclude ...'; so that for all I knew there was a tablet bearing my name on the church wall by now. How awkward it was coming back from the dead. No wonder Stetson had been so put out. But it would be easier with my sister: I would not shock her with a cable but would send her a long, soothing letter. She wouldn't have time to reply, but that didn't matter. She would have been prepared ... and gently. I would tell her to keep my mail and to expect me in about ten days—I should be flown home, Stetson said—and that I should warn her as soon as I reached London.

So I wrote to my sister; then I settled to my report for Stetson; and nine days later I left by air for home.

And so now at last I was to see them all again—the only family I had. My sister Anne, Richard her husband, my nephew (and my godson) Robin. Robin had been five when I left in 1943, a merry, bubbling infant; now he would be nine, gravely dressed in grey shorts and knee-stockings, rather reserved I anticipated, in his smart prep. school blazer. Very different from the trusting baby who had trotted round the room in his blue pyjamas on my last night at home.

'Robin can stay up a little longer,' Anne had said. 'This is a special occasion.'

'Yes,' said Richard; 'we must have a bottle of the 1912.'

On any special occasion, grave or gay, Richard would open a bottle or two of the famous 1912. There had been, Richard would say, no year to equal it. If only his father had realized soon enough and bought more. . . . I remembered how, on that distant evening in 1943, he had said:

'I've only a dozen left now. But I shall save a bottle for the day you come back.'

'When *will* uncle Jonathan come back?' asked Robin.

'Quite soon,' I said.

'How soon is quite soon?'

'When the war's over. The time will pass very quickly.'

'Sometimes it does,' said Robin reflectively, 'sometimes not. What makes the time go slow and then suddenly fast?'

'You'll be busy,' I said, 'busy learning things at school. Time always goes fast for busy people.'

'Will *you* be busy, Uncle Jonathan?'

'I expect so.'

'So the time will go fast for both of us till Uncle Jonathan comes home again. Robin is very glad,' said Robin.

Then he gave me a hug and a kiss and was taken away to bed by Anne.

'The government is going to take this place over as a hospital,' Richard had said later, gently tilting the decanter of 1912 over my glass. 'I'm not really too upset. It's very difficult for Anne just now with no servants and Robin at a demanding age. It's next August they're coming, I think.'

'Where will you live?'

'I'm having a sort of flat done up over the stables. It wasn't easy to arrange—the work permits and so on were endless— but they agreed finally because I shall still be farming the land. It'll be quite comfortable and I shall still be living more or less in my own home. And if things go well after the war, perhaps we can move back.'

'Government concerns are like women. Easy to get into a house, impossible to get out.'

Richard laughed.

'We want no cynicism from departing heroes,' he said.

Then Anne rejoined us.

'Robin is asleep,' she said. 'He put Uncle Jonathan before Mummy and Daddy in his prayers tonight. Afterwards he told me it was just this once, because Uncle Jonathan was going away to the war.'

And two big tears had rolled slowly down her cheeks.

This, then, was the family to which I was returning after so long. My sister Anne, her gentle husband with his cherished

acres of Kentish soil, and my nephew Robin—now, I must
suppose, an unknown quantity. And, of course, the last bottle
of 1912. How wonderful it would be to sit with them all again,
above the stables or perhaps in the old house itself, hearing
Richard's quiet voice tell of the crops or the summer's cricket,
persuading Robin to take me back into his life and to talk of
his school and his friends, and drinking the noblest of all wines
from Anne's beautiful glass. I was not ashamed that I thought
almost as much of the wine as of the people I loved, for the
bottle of wine had become a symbol to me as the years went on.
It was the symbol of my return; when it appeared, cradled in
Richard's careful hands, it would be a sign that the years of pain
were finally done and that at last and for ever I was home. What
more seemly offering to the returning soldier and what more
fitting object for his thoughts? Wine, that maketh glad the heart
of a man.

My aeroplane was punctual, but in London I came up against
a mild difficulty. I had promised in my letter from Delhi to warn
Anne as soon as I reached England. Enquiring from the telephone exchange, I found that Richard's house was now listed
as —— Hospital, and that they had no number for Richard
himself, whom I must presume was still living with Anne above
the stables. That Richard should not be listed was really natural
enough, because at the time when he had the stables done up
to live in, neither love nor money could procure private tele-
phones and this, according to the exchange, was still the case.
But how to warn Anne? I toyed with the idea of ringing the
Hospital and asking them to take over a message, but did not
fancy talking to some sniffish Matron who would make me feel
she was being put upon. In the end I dictated a wire, incurring
some expense by making it elaborately plain in the address that
the recipient lived in an annexe of the Hospital. I should be
arriving by train, I told Anne, at nine-thirty that night.

There was no one to meet me at the station (no petrol? Had
that wretched wire misfired after all my trouble?), so I took a
taxi to the gate of the park where, having only a small case, I

yielded to a sentimental impulse and paid off the driver. I would walk up the drive, I thought, at once delaying and giving spice to the arrival I had dreamed of so often. Although it had been dark some time, there was a fair three-quarter moon and I could relish the familiar trees and hedges. At first I was surprised to find myself walking, not on gravel, but on concrete; then I remembered that government hospitals have money to spend. I hoped they had not spent too much, for I cared little for alteration, let it be a cause that was never so excellent. On the whole I was reassured. There were two or three shapeless huts in the fields on either side, but perhaps Richard would find them useful when the hospital left or be able to remove them. And as I approached the house, I saw that its low and graceful front, long and white and welcoming, was the same as ever; save for a couple of ambulances parked at the bottom of the steps nothing indicated disturbance or even change. Inside of course ... But I could hear about that later. Now I must go to my family. To the bottle of 1912. I turned along a wall, went through a door, stepped into the stable yard. And there to greet me, with his head sticking out of a window above the stables, was my nephew Robin.

'Uncle Jonathan,' he called, 'uncle Jonathan.'

'Robin,' I said, 'oh, Robin.'

'I knew you were coming,' he called.

'You had my telegram all right?'

'I knew you were coming. Go through that door in front of you and up the stairs. I'm in the first room at the top.'

I opened the door and, with some difficulty, picked my way up the narrow and uncarpeted stairway. War-time work, I thought; shoddy. But there was nothing shoddy or uncomfortable about the room in which I found my nephew. There was a polished table and a bright fire. Robin himself was standing near the window, behind a beautifully covered sofa which I remembered from the house in the old days. He had grown up splendidly, my godson. Straight fair hair, a round, honest face with a clear if slightly pale complexion. Bright eyes. A sound, well-proportioned build, suggesting that he was ten or eleven rather than nine. Robin had always been big for his age. He made a handsome figure standing there behind the sofa in his blue pyjamas, allowed to wait up—how else on such a night— to welcome his uncle home.

'I've waited so long for you to come,' he said, 'to welcome you back from the war. And then today they told me you were coming.'

'I took a lot of trouble to address the telegram right,' I said.

Then I waited for him to come to me. He did not move. Boys of nine dislike demonstration, I thought, they don't want to be kissed and mauled about even by mothers and long-lost uncles. He is shy, reserved, as I knew he would be. Let him come in his own time.

'Where are Mummy and Daddy?' I asked.

'I always knew you were all right,' he said; 'I knew you would come back.'

I could wait no longer.

'Then come and shake hands with me, Robin. Let me have a look at you.'

Still he did not move.

'I knew you would come back. The wine is ready for you.'

He pointed to a small side table. On it stood a decanter, gleaming, purple, imperial, and by it one of Anne's most beautiful glasses, into which some wine had already been poured.

'The 1912?' I asked. 'The last bottle?'

'Yes, Uncle Jonathan. The last bottle. Now you must drink.'

'But where are Mummy and Daddy? I must wait for them.'

'They don't want you to wait, Uncle Jonathan.'

'Then surely you will drink with me, Robin? You are a big chap now. A small glass won't harm you.'

'No, thank you, Uncle Jonathan. But you must drink.'

So I lifted the full glass that stood on the table and raised it in front of my face.

'To you, Robin,' I said, 'to my nephew and godson, who has grown into such a fine boy.'

'Thank you, Uncle Jonathan,' he said.

I sipped the wine. For a moment the magnificent flavour, first deep and distant, then rich, then subtly apologetic for its richness, bringing the assurance that life was good and God was merciful, was there as it always had been. Then I was alone in a cold, bare room, with only the moon to shine on the cracked and filthy glass in my hand and with a taste of vinegar and ashes on my tongue.

At the reception desk of the hospital they gave me my bundle of letters, the letters which had followed me to Delhi and had been sent back to my next of kin in Kent. There were only a few from Anne and Richard, and one scrawl in capitals from Robin, at the bottom of the pile. Above these was the buff envelope, and the sheets of thin war-time paper inside it, which told how they had all three been killed, in the late summer of 1943, when a braking ambulance skidded off the gravel drive and crashed into them where they stood by the park gate.

THE AMATEUR

'What about a trip to the September meeting at Perth?' I said.

'No,' said Rollo Rutupium very firmly; 'not Perth.'

'Why not? It's one of the most attractive courses in the kingdom.'

'So I used to think,' said Rollo; 'I changed my mind.'

'Why?'

Rollo thought heavily for half a minute.

'Once upon a time,' he said at last, 'I had an affair with a very appetising undergraduate in Trinity Hall.'

'What's she got to do with it?'

'He. This was over forty years ago . . . before all those women shoved themselves in where they weren't wanted.'

'Oh, come on Rollo,' I said. 'It must be rather jolly there now, with plenty of girls around.'

'There was plenty forty years ago, if you knew where to look. The thing was that they all had their own colleges and had to go back to them for most of the time. A man could get away from them if he wanted to. They weren't in one's room giggling and whining and demanding and wearing out the furniture all day and all night—which is what it's like now, my nephews tell me.'

'Well, that's their worry. This catamite of yours in Trinity Hall—what's he got to do with Perth Race Course?'

'He wasn't a catamite, for a start. A catamite is a boy whom you bugger. Although I have always been in favour of widely varying sexual practice with all the genders, I absolutely drew a line at buggery. Messy, painful, and (as it now turns out) potentially lethal.'

'All right,' I said: 'this fancy boy of yours. What's he got to do with Per—'

'He wasn't a fancy boy either. Definitely not mincing or dainty. He was butch and wholesome and just a little bit bandy. Played cricket and rugger for Trinity Hall. Blue eyes and Viking blond hair and a slightly snub nose. Medium height. When he played tennis in white shorts, his bonny bow legs (smooth as silk) used to flash and twinkle all over the court like magic.'

'Steady on,' I said: 'that's enough.'

'No it isn't,' said Rollo. 'If you want to appreciate this story, you must first know all about Micky. Micky Ruck, he was called. I sat next to him by accident in one of Professor Adcock's lectures on the late Roman Republic. Adders was buzzing away about that crook, Clodius, and suddenly there we were, Micky and I, playing footsie and kneesie and thighsie like a pair of demented fourth formers ... Mind you, I was quite a dish myself in those days. Tall and languid and sinuous ... hardly a hair anywhere on my body, except a small blob of pert pubes.'

'Love at first sight?'

'No love about it. Sheer randiness. Yearning for flesh and skin. But there *was* affection. I enjoyed his sort of accommodating naivety, while he admired my upper class demeanour and cynicism. So in no time at all we were lusty bedfellows—he used to laugh a lot, I remember, just before he came—and excellent occasional companions, playing squash and watching cricket at Fenner's. However there was just one cloud in the sky.'

'Scandal?'

'No. We usually met in my own college, King's, and in King's in those days nobody worried about that kind of carry-on. However, the trouble was that Micky was afraid that because he liked doing it with other boys he might turn into a full-time homosexual. The Classics master at his school, unlike the Classics master at mine, hadn't pointed out to him that the norm both in Greece and Rome, at any rate among the best people, was an easy going bisexuality. So I now made this plain to him, quoting chapter and verse, and just to set his mind at rest I arranged for my cousin, Heather Sopworth of Girton, to give him a go. As I told you just now, you could always find a girl if you needed one, even then . . . long before they infested the entire University.'

'And how did he get on with Heather Sopworth?'

'Spiffing. Heather was a grand girl, as I knew well enough; we'd been intimate playmates since we were twelve. She told Micky that he was the best she'd ever had except me, and explained that a taste for boys made boys far more attractive to girls (jealousy and curiosity) and also made girls far more attractive (by sheer contrast) to boys. He could have the best of all possible worlds, she told him, but he should remember that he had only a limited time in which to enjoy them: boys will be boys, but not for long. When he became a man, she said, he'd probably still be pretty attractive, but by then women might expect him to be faithful to them, or even to marry them, and that would be a bore. So gather ye rosebuds while ye may, Heather urged, on both sides of the garden path.'

'I still don't see,' I said, 'what any of this has to do with Perth.'

'Patience,' Rollo said. 'So Micky was gathering rosebuds in all directions, Heather's and mine and God knows who else's, when it occurred to me one May morning that I should be going down for good in June, after which I should have National Service for two years, much of it very likely abroad, and that there would be an end of Micky Ruck. I therefore decided to extend my stay in Paradise by arranging a last spree with Micky the following August and September, before he must go back to Cambridge and I myself must list for a temporary lancer. Micky and I would have a Grand Sporting Tour, taking in Festival Cricket Weeks—there were plenty of those then, before the game was put in charge of a money-grubbing inquisition from the Corporals' Mess—and lots of tennis tournaments, both real tennis and lawners, and plenty of golf and racing. We could start at Lord's, make our way up through England and then Scotland to Gleneagles, and then on to the goal and crown of the whole expedition, the September Meeting (here we are at last) at Perth.'

'Bravo,' I said.

'One possible obstacle, however, was Micky's adoring Mum, who liked her little boy to be with her during the hols. Luckily she was a howling snob. I hadn't inherited then but she knew who I was, so to speak—Micky never really understood all that, bless his heart—and she was very pleased with our friendship. As for the idea that something might be going on, it didn't bother her. She wasn't fussy. I did have to pay a toll of a night in bed with her—but it was no trouble. Like her son, she roared with laughter when she was coming; and she kept on calling me "Micky darling" by mistake, which had interesting and rather exciting implications. Anyway, I soon had her *imprimatur* for our journey.

'And so off we went, Micky and I, in that Lagonda I used to have, playing in the odd match for the Butterflies and IZ—Micky belonged to neither but a few smiles at the right people soon settled that problem—watching the late county games, going to early National Hunt meetings at Hereford and Stratford and Sedgefield (proper country meetings, none of those pimply pimps and lacquered whores that you get at the meetings near London), popping in at Doncaster for a bit of flat, di-da, di-da, some tennis (Royal) at Chester and some Shakespeare in Edinburgh, until at last we came to Perth, where we put up at a very decent pub in the forest some miles north of the course.

'We had a day spare before the racing started, and so, since Micky was getting into one of his periodical states about being too queer—he'd been laughing like a satyr all the way from London and was afraid he was enjoying himself too much—I took him to see Penny Pertuis, a busty widow whose husband had been in the same regiment as my father. Penny was a versatile lady who now taught anthropology at the University of St Andrews; she showed us round the golf course as far as the ninth, where we retired into the bushes for a picnic followed by a tremendous three ball. I let Micky do most of the fornicating, to restore his confidence, and what with him laughing and Penny bawling obscenities, which was her way of showing gratitude, I thought we'd have the entire Committee of the Royal and Ancient charging down on us like a Squadron of the Greys. But no, we were only spotted by a red-headed Scots laddie looking for lost balls to sell, who happily made up a foursome—nothing so rorty as a wee ginger Scot.

'Blissfully tired after a long day in the fresh air, we set out back towards Perth, taking Penny, who had decided to come to the races with us the next day. We telephoned the pub to book her in and order our dinner, and on the way back we paid a visit to the Palace at Scone. Although the place had just closed when we reached it, Penny knew a private way in, and in any case the purpose of our call was not to see the Palace itself but to inspect a remarkable graveyard they have there, in the woods near the Chapel, because Penny the Anthropologist had some theory about eighteenth-century burials in that part of the world and she had heard that there might be something helpful there at Scone.

'Now Penny's theory had to do with the sepulchral use of the obelisk. There was, so they said, a particularly fine obelisk at one end of this very grave ground, an obelisk which had been put up over the remains of one Purvis Pride, the eldest son of Purvis Pride the Pride of Birnam, the Prides, then as now, being great men in the county and devils for hunting. The Pride under the obelisk had been killed steeplechasing in 1789, at the age of nineteen . . . this during a cross country race which had started in the hills up at Belbeggie and ended (so Penny told us) at a tavern which then stood by a copse in the middle of the meadow that formed the centre of the modern circuit. Young Purvis, when well in the lead, had broken his neck at the last obstacle of all—the stream in which the good woman of the tavern did her washing. She'd hung a huge night shirt out on a hedge to dry, and the wind had got up and blown it straight on to horse and rider, blinding them both just as they were about to jump the steeply banked stream. The horse, a stallion called Jupiter Tonans, had perished with Purvis and was buried with him.

'Penny's theory' (Rollo went on) 'was that obelisks were reserved for the remains of gallant men—soldiers and sailors, explorers and adventurers. What she wanted was to read the inscription on the Pride obelisk, which was said to include a phrase which would explain why Purvis Pride, a mere local huntsman and stripling amateur jockey, had been allowed the full funereal apparatus of a proven man of action.

'Having climbed a bolted postern in the wall which ran parallel to the Perth-Balmoral road, we approached the burial ground through graceful conifers and along a sunken path. This opened out in a delta at the east end of the cemetery, where the trees gave way to the ranked monuments. Although evening had not yet fallen, the grave ground in front of us (about one hundred yards by fifty) was diffusing its own shade of subfusc illumination from the lolling mounds and crumbling pedestals, the black slabs and sweaty cylinders which made up the assembly of seventeenth- and eighteenth-century sepulture. We filed through the stones, Penny leading, Micky and I, seeing as little as possible of the spikes and balls and skulking crosses, until we came to the far end, the end nearest the Chapel (which was just visible through high bush and ladybirch) and the Palace itself, about a furlong beyond, on the far side of a broad, trim lawn. But our attention was soon distracted both from the Chapel and Palace by the grave which we had come to see. A marble obelisk, of a tall man's height and topped by what looked like a mortarboard without its tassel, stood on a small grass island which was surrounded by a moat of dark water about seven foot wide.

' "Apparently it's quite deep," said Penny: "not for wading. And anyone that jumped it would break his napper on the obelisk. Luckily I can read the inscription from here with my race glasses."

'She took these from their case . . . the ones her husband had used all through Italy.

' "Take it down," she told me, and glinted through the glasses at the inscription on the side of the obelisk which was facing us.

' " 'Brave rider, Purvis Pride,' " she read, " 'Brave stallion had to ride; *Jupiter Tonans* him did call, who slew both by cursed fall.' Not a high standard of verse," observed Penny. "But there's a bit more—in Latin. '*Nonne quidem stuporum poenitet animum equitis hic sepulti in saecula saeculorum cum nobilitate equi sui.*' Interesting use of the abstract: 'the nobleness of his horse' instead of 'his noble horse'."

' "In sum," translated Micky, looking over my shoulder at the transcript. "Surely the soul of the horseman repents of his *stuprorum*—debaucheries—buried here as he is for ever with his noble horse?" Informing us that the horse, *Jupiter Tonans*, is in there too.'

' "That we knew," said Penny, "though it is useful to have it confirmed. The glowing tribute to *Jupiter Tonans* obviously explains why Purvis Pride's tomb was dignified with an obelisk. Clearly the obelisk is for 'the noble horse' rather than his rider. But there remains a slight mystery: it seems that Purvis was guilty of certain *stupra* of which, it is hoped, he will repent at leisure, perhaps influenced in this by his 'noble' companion. Evidently these *stupra* were considered no great matter; otherwise this memorial would not have been allowed an obelisk in the first place however great the fame and nobility of *Jupiter Tonans*. The nice question is, *exactly* what were they, these *stupra*? Micky has translated them as 'debaucheries', but what specific debaucheries?" '

' "The word is commonly used both in Latin prose and verse," said Micky the classicist, "of any sexual misdemeanour and in particular of orgies or adulteries. Perhaps Purvis Pride junior went round tumbling the local wives? Not much of a crime for a well-connected young man in the eighteenth century."

' "A considerable crime in Scotland," said Penny. "The Kirk would not have stood for it ... and would certainly not have permitted him this kind of interment in this kind of place."

' "No doubt," I myself put in, "Father Pride the Pride of Birnam had a liberal palm for greasing other palms. Come to that, the Kirk or the Episcopalians—whichever administrated this place—might not have been too keen on a bloody great stallion being permitted Christian burial."

' "Good point," said Penny: "a nice fat bribe covers the difficulties all round. No doubt Father Purvis squared it for both of them—for *Jupiter Tonans* and for little Purvis."

' "It would still be amusing," said Micky, "to know precisely what he squared in the way of *stuprorum*. He stooped down and looked into the black moat. "Purvis Pride, Purvis Pride," he intoned, "what naughtiness did *you* get up to?"

'Answer came there none, except for Penny's comment: "Pretty boys should not go close to still waters. Remember little Greek Hylas, who was hauled in by the Water Nymphs."

' "They don't have Water Nymphs in Scotland," Micky said: "the Kirk would never allow it." '

★　★　★

'The next day,' continued Rollo, 'we all went to Perth Races. The Course, as you know, is not far from Scone; indeed if you stand by the second jump out from Tattersall's you can see a bit of a rampart or whatever through the trees which separate the circuit from the Palace gardens. So here we came and stood for the big race, a very long steeplechase during which the horses and their riders would take this fence three times.

' "You will observe," said Penny as we walked across the meadow from the Enclosure, "that the Purvis family is well represented. Purvis Pride—surely a descendant—is to ride his gelding, Long John Silver. Black and White halved with Black Cap."

' "Same colours as the Hall," Micky said. "Trinity Hall," he explained to Penny, "my college. We call it the Hall for short."

' "So I surmised," said Penny.

' "Of course I've backed him," bubbled Micky. "The layers gave me a hundred quid to a tenner."

' "Extravagant boy."

' "It's well worth a tenner," Micky said, "just to be standing here in this lovely place."

'One quite saw what he meant' (Rollo pursued). 'In front of us, the other side of the course, were the trees up the gentle slope to the peeping Palace; behind us was the meadow and two hundred yards away the copse near which had stood the vanished tavern, by a stream that had also vanished, where the eighteenth-century Purvis Pride had broken his neck. Beyond the far end of the course the countryside idled away, pine and bracken, to a semi-circle of low hills. " 'What are those blue remembered hills','" I quoted, " 'What spires, what farms, are those?' " " 'This is the land of lost content'," murmured Micky, continuing Housman's poem, while a single tear ran down the left side of Penny Pertuis's nose.

' "Pay attention to the racing, boys," she said huskily.

' "THEY'RE OFF."

'It cannot be said that young Purvis Pride's Long John Silver distinguished himself. Nor did his rider. A series of blunders, the first of them at the fence by which we were standing, soon put him a good twenty lengths behind the rest of the small field (seven in all). The second time round he was trailing even further; but he managed to stay upright for a further circuit, and as he went past us for the third and last time he appeared to be rallying slightly and drawing nearer to the pack of six horses in front. When the field emerged from behind the copse, with half a mile to run, Long John Silver had come level with the last horse and seemed to be making good ground. Over the last ditch, with two plain fences still to jump, he was lying fourth ... but thereafter reverted to his previous form, sagged back to the rear of what was now a forlorn queue. Ye Banks and Braes, the only mare in the race, was going to win by a corridor: Long John Silver passed the post last by thirty lengths.

' "So much for my tenner," said Micky; "boring race."

' "I don't know," said Penny. "For a time he quickened rather bravely. Then something took the heart out of him."

' "I don't think there was ever much heart there."

' "He seems to be showing a bit more now," Penny said.

'And indeed, having barely flopped past the post, Long John Silver with Purvis on his back in his black and white colours had started to gallop again and was coming very fast round the bend and towards the fence at which we were still standing.

' "He's riding very long," said Micky. "I didn't notice that before."

' "Perhaps he's lost his stirrups," I said.

' "No," said Penny. "He's riding long." She concentrated through her glasses as horse and jockey drew closer. "And he isn't riding Long John Silver," Penny squawked, "he's riding a stallion, dear Jesus – "

'—The stallion veered to its right, jumped the rails between the course and the meadow, set straight at us, came swiftly closer. The rider, a wedge-faced youth with a shapeless black cap and no helmet, leant down and across, seized Micky by the scruff of his jacket, tensed and hauled him up like a circus act. He wheeled his horse (Micky now being bunched in front of him like a parcel), jumped back on to the race course, then over the hedge on the far side, and galloped away through the scattered clumps towards Scone.

' "Now we know," said Penny, shivering and jerking, "what form Purvis Pride's *stupra* took. The dead Purvis Pride. I told Micky he shouldn't have looked into that moat. You see what's happened?"

' "I think so." I retched. "It must have cost the Pride of Birnam a pretty penny in bribes to arrange for that monument—if his son's tastes were known when he was living."

' "They must have been known. *Stupra*. Abomination. Perhaps they thought he would be ... safer ... in consecrated ground. Perhaps they forced his father ... to add an obelisk to keep him down ... a moat to keep him in ... just in case, they thought. Just in case."

' "What now?" I said. "Shall we go to the graveyard?"

' "No point," Penny said. "We can't compete ..."

'Nevertheless we did go there. And saw nothing we had not

seen the day before. The waters of the moat were dark and still as ever. We went back to the pub—what else could we do?—and ordered dinner.

*   *   *

'Half way through dinner,' said Rollo, 'Micky came back. He was shrivelled and yellow and taut. He ate ferociously, and didn't talk till he had finished. Even then he spoke mostly in monosyllables, at once clear, courteous and impersonal, as if he did not know to whom he was speaking, as if he were the voice of an answering machine. He named neither of us and made no reference to what had occurred, beyond saying, "I am there. We must go to me there. You must take me to me."

' "Now?" asked Penny.

' "Tomorrow," stated what was left of Micky Ruck.

'And so the next morning we took him there to him. We called his name. Poor, shrunken Micky leant over the moat, while Penny and I stood discreetly just behind him. "Micky, Micky Ruck," Micky called. His reflection appeared in the dark water, the reflection of a rosy, laughing boy with blond hair and a snub nose, full of jollity and juice.

' "Micky, Micky Ruck," Micky called.

'But the reflection laughed the more, waved happily, and faded.

' "Please take me away," said Micky to Penny and me, as if he were addressing two complete strangers and asking for a lift.

'And now you know,' said Rollo Rutupium, 'Why I shall not, if you will kindly excuse me, be accompanying you to the September meeting at Perth.'

THE PROSELYTE

'Odd,' I said to my friend Decimus, 'the French don't usually leave their cemeteries unlocked.'

'Odder still,' Decimus said, 'this one is a meadow of grass, like an English churchyard. Normally the French have a barrack square of tarmac with huge and hideous hunks of concrete jutting out of it . . . and obligatory ranks of cypress round the edge. Here, you notice, there are additional rows of cypress to form an avenue, direct from this gate and up the middle of the cemetery, all the way to that monstrous tomb at the far end.'

'Clearly,' I said, 'one is expected to walk along the avenue and examine the Monument.'

The village was called Unac. Some way off the road between Ax-les-Thermes and Foix, it lay concealed in a fold on the south-west slope of a steep ridge. To reach it one had to take a sly turning off the main road, then pass through the installations of a Cement Works, which was smugly polluting the River Ariege just below it, then up and up through dense, scrubby woods and along a deserted byway, until one came to a Romanesque Church with a fine but tottery Tower which displayed rows of twelfth century arches in all four sides and at three upper levels.

A little further on was an inn of ancient exterior but adequate appointment. Here we had taken rooms, and were now exploring the village. There seemed to be no one in it, until we came to the Church, seemly and restful without, full of idle, chattering boys and old women fiercely dusting simpering madonnas within. No one took any notice of us, and presently we had moved on a quarter of a mile up the empty road to the cemetery.

As we paced slowly along the avenue of cypress towards the Monument at its end, Decimus said:

'After the boy had shown me to my room and dumped my bags, he was keen to converse in English.'

'How touching. And how tedious. I wondered what was keeping you.'

'The boy showed me a miniature bottle on my bed table. It contained some liquid of a delicate pink, and was labelled "Eau de Vie de Tarascon". The boy explained to me that this was not the tourist town on the Rhone near Arles and Avignon, but Tarascon-sur-Ariege, distinguished for its congregation of the Albigensian sect—Cathars, as they are often called—some few leagues from Unac. He said that there had been a cask of this Eau de Vie de Tarascon in the cellar of our pub for as long as anyone could remember, but at last it had been decided to tap the cask and bottle the content, some of which was put into miniatures for the guests' bedrooms.'

'There was none in mine,' I said.

'The boy then went on to say that Unac had been a hiding place for Cathar heretics (as the Roman Church branded them) from Tarascon and other towns during de Montfort's anti-Cathar Crusade from the north. And after that too, the boy said.'

'He seems to have been a very well informed boy. Mine was the village imbecile.'

'So remote was Unac, my boy said, that Cathars had been safe here. Then that beastly Cement Works had come and drawn people off to live down below. But there were still a few of the faithful left in Unac. The village *abbé*, he told me, was a secret Cathar—a *parfait*, or *perfectus*. You know what that means?'

'Very roughly, that he has forsworn all the pleasures of this world, which is the Creation of the Devil.'

'That's about it,' said Decimus. 'No meat, or even fish, no alcohol, no sex; just vegetables, which should be raw, and water. That didn't apply to ordinary Cathars of course. Ordinary Cathars do pretty much as they please—until they are on their deathbed. Then they are purged by a *perfectus* in order to ensure their salvation and an immediate passage to Paradise.'

'How very convenient for them. I wonder,' I said, 'what that monument is all about. Two of those old women from the Church are arranging flowers there.'

'It was free,' said Decimus.

'What was?'

'That Eau de Vie de Tarascon. It was a gift from the hotel, the boy told me; a welcome to Unac.'

'Was it indeed? Why wasn't there any in my room?'

'An oversight, I expect. Or perhaps,' said Decimus, quite seriously, 'they didn't think you deserved any.'

The two women by the Monument had just been joined by a Priest who wore a rough black cloak and voluminous, ungainly shoes.

'As if I care,' I said. 'I don't trust these regional concoctions. They give me indigestion. Did you taste the stuff?'

'Oh yes. It seemed the polite thing to do. It didn't,' said Decimus, 'taste at all like Eau de Vie.'

'If it's old enough, it wouldn't taste of anything. Have you ever drunk genuine Napoleon Cognac—distilled during his reign? Its entire essence has been murdered by time.'

'This tasted of something all right. Thick and mushy. Saline. The boy was very pleased when I drank it.'

'Did you ask why it tasted so odd?'

'Yes. He said it was an acquired taste.'

'Cathars,' I said; 'Albigensians ... Let me think ... Yes. There was a book about them, about those that survived the Crusade of de Montfort, called *Montaillou*. It said, among much else, that when a Cathar died, the Priest, the *Parfait* or *Perfectus* who was in attendance, cut off some extremity from the body—a finger, a toe, a nose or an ear, sometimes even the *privata*. Such ... such tokens were kept in the house to guarantee that the strength and spirit of the dead man should survive and bring prosperity to those he had loved. The remnants were preserved in vials or vessels of salt water, which was sprinkled about the precincts, now and then, in ritual blessing. Some of this water was then imbibed by members of the family, and the container re-charged with salt and liquid . . . until the next time. A strictly non-alcoholic beverage you see—fit for consumption by *parfaits* and by their purged disciples who were aspiring to salvation and the Cathar Paradise . . . Eau de Vie de Tarascon.'

The women, having finished their flower arrangement, now left the Monument and came towards us. The priest, who had been facing it, turned round but stood quite still. The boy who had carried up Decimus's bags in the hotel now appeared from behind the Monument, dressed in the rough brown cape of a shepherd, and stood behind and just to the right of the Priest, who inclined and slightly turned his head, and began to murmur in French:

'What was the name of the donor?'

'Pierre Maury,' the boy answered. '1778.'

The women took hold of Decimus, gently but very firmly, one gripping his left arm, the other the right. On the Monument, I now saw, were several columns of names, often the name of Maury, with dates which started in 1097 and ended in 1988. The marble of the Monument, now that I was looking at it from fairly close to, no longer seemed monstrous. It was in the form of a slightly irregular tetrahedron, which brooded (but without menace) in its own place, silently and massively self-assured. The carving of the letters and numbers was clear and delicate, all columns being of the same length except for the one on the right, which was still unfinished and ended with an entry for 1988.

'And our brother's name?' said the Priest.

'The passport he carried,' said the boy, 'was of Decimus Alastair Constant Rumbold.'

'You may go now,' said the Priest to me, in soft, correct English. 'Your friend will be fully attended to and made welcome.'

Decimus's head was drooping; he appeared to have fainted or fallen asleep. 'See how he is at peace,' said the Priest. 'He has partaken of the spirit of Pierre Maury; many of us are of that family; he has nothing to fear. Nor, if you are his true friend, need you grieve for him.'

'FOR CHRIST'S SAKE,' I mouthed.

'No,' said the Priest, 'for God's sake, and God's love. You must rejoice that your friend has been chosen.'

The passing bell began to ring from the Tower. A coffin was carried up the avenue of cypress by some of the boys who had been chattering so gaily in the Church. There was no lid.

'It is better if you go now,' the Priest said courteously.

A merciful dark came upon me.

★   ★   ★

When I awoke in my hotel bed, the imbecile boy, who had shown me up on my first arrival, was standing over me with a tray of coffee. He put this down, then pointed to my clock. The hands stood at midnight. The boy drew the curtains. Bright sunshine. Not midnight: noon. I had slept for seventeen hours.

'My friend?' I said, 'Mister Rumbold?'

The boy shook his head as if I were the imbecile.

Later I walked to the cemetery and to the Monument. At the bottom of the right hand column of names there was now one more: Decimus Alastair Constant Rumbold 1989.

Why Decimus? I thought. Why not me too? Simply thank God, I thought, and go. Then I remembered the courtesy and the dignity of the Priest, the gentleness of the old women, the intelligent face of the boy who had been Decimus's teacher and (I suppose) his sponsor at the end. A *parfait* or *perfectus*, I remembered again, is one who has rejected the pleasures of this World, which was created by the Devil. But Cathars—the Pure Ones (as the word, Greek in origin, declares them)—did not want me, and I must go.

I returned to the inn, seeing nobody on the way. The door stood open; my luggage was neatly arranged at the bottom of the stairs. I called several times, but there was no answer. At least, I thought, as I drove through the empty streets and turned down towards the Cement Works, I have had no bill to pay; the Cathars' final courtesy to a superfluous guest.

THE CADDY

'This is Martin Lash,' said the lean Brigadier, 'from Holland. I knew you wouldn't mind a three-ball.'

I hate three-balls, as my face made very plain.

'We must not be selfish,' said the lean Brigadier, flexing one shank and then the other under his plus-twos; 'we must be civil to foreigners: common market and all that crap. But you needn't worry what you say in front of him. Rather unusually for an educated Dutchman, he does not speak English. Just smile at him from time to time—that's all I'm asking.'

'That and a three-ball,' I said, grinning thinly at Martin Lash: 'he'll hold us up like the very devil.'

'Oh no. I'm getting him a caddy. You don't want one, I take it?'

'I can't afford one.'

'Good. I thought not. It would have been inconvenient.'

'Inconvenient?'

'I'm not having one either', said the Brigadier, 'although I usually do. You'll see why later on.'

Martin Lash was one of those men like a barrel surmounted by a croquet ball and supported by two buckets. He had been turning a polite po-face from one to the other of us during our conversation, but now showed signs of becoming restive.

'Let's get on with it,' said the Brigadier, as if duty and not pleasure were in prospect. He waved a hand towards the Caddy Master's hut. A wiry ephebe emerged: he wore a long and ragged black jerkin of indeterminate material above baggy grey trousers which ended just below the knee: his calves and feet were bare.

'This is Saul Bax,' said the Brigadier: and to Lash, 'Saul ... Bax ... Caddy.'

Bax very slightly bowed his bullet head. Lash, who seemed to have got the message, nodded his appreciation and handed his very heavy and elaborate bag to sinewy (perhaps sixteen years old) Saul Bax.

'Showy foreign rubbish,' said the Brigadier.

'Aye, Master,' said Saul Bax.

We played the first, a short par 4, towards some ugly breeding boxes (the only nasty sight on the course) which marked the end of the town. The brigadier was keeping a card: Lash had a 4 at the first (a very lucky one), the Brigadier had a 5, and I had a scruffy 6. So Lash had the honour on the second tee, where we now turned and began to play away from the breeders (in a northerly direction towards Sandwich), having the first fairway on our left and the sea shore on our right. Lash sliced heavily. His ball ballooned up against the East Wind and fell, almost abreast of where we stood but a long way from us, on to the pebbled beach.

'You go with Mr Lash, Saul,' said the Brigadier after both he and I had managed to drive moderately straight, 'and try to find his ball. No point the rest of us coming.'

'Aye, Master,' said Bax.

When we were alone, the Brigadier started to become conspiratorial.

'Met him in Amsterdam,' he said. 'Interesting name. Invited him over.'

'Who is that caddy?' I said. 'Is he too skint to buy shoes, poor chap?'

'On the contrary, Saul Bax is very well provided for,' said the lean Brigadier, swaying from his pins to his crackly physog in the east wind which blew from the sea.

'For that very reason he doesn't often work here, and so you won't have seen him before. As for his feet, I suppose he likes to go with them bare.' He paused. 'Lee shore this morning: splendid day for wrecking.'

'For what?'

'You surely knew that the inhabitants of this coast were

famous for wrecking? You're a literary chap—Defoe says a great deal about it in his *Tour Round the Island of Great Britain*. When ships were driven ashore on a day like today, the gangs would turn out from Walmer, Deal and Sandwich and butcher the crews for the booty. By the end of the seventeenth century the law got a bit of a hold: but residual gangs of wreckers operated from the dunes and the marshes until the end of the eighteenth century and even later.'

Martin Lash and Saul Bax reappeared. Both shook their heads. At the end of the second hole the Brigadier scored a 5 for himself and me, and a dash for Lash.

'What system are you using to score?' I asked.

'It doesn't much matter. Just filling this in for the sake of it.'

'We might at least be serious about the match,' I said, 'even if it is a three-ball.'

'Oh yes. We're very serious indeed. You'll see. Won't he, Saul?' the Brigadier called to Bax.

'Aye, Master,' said Bax.

As the round proceeded, Lash, who was plainly not used to such conditions, became wilder and wilder in his strokes. Whithersoever he propelled his ball, the faithful Bax went with him, and was surprisingly often successful in finding it. During these interludes the Brigadier continued his account of the local wreckers.

'Out of the dunes,' he said. 'Leaving a look-out in case the Excise Men stuck their noses in—out of the dunes, on to the beach, hack the sailormen to bits with old iron and cutlasses—Russians, Germans, French, Dutch, or even English, what the hell?—and fetch the loot back into the marshes just down the coast, between here and Sandwich. It must have been just such a day as this in late August, 1782—warmer of course but just as windy. This time they set a woman to watch, as they sometimes did when men were short. I'll show you where they posted her, later.'

Lash and Bax rejoined us. Lash was allowed to drop his ball

and we all played up from a dip (mercifully windless) on to a plateau green on a bank which merged into the beach. Lash held a single putt.

'Give him 4 then,' said the Brigadier; 'as I say, it doesn't much matter.'

From the next tee, which was adjacent to the previous green, Lash hooked with the wind off the sea. He and Bax tramped into a wilderness of long, spiked grasses.

'One of the crew escaped,' said the Brigadier. 'He ran over this very spot. Desperate. No golf course then. Just that cling-ing, spiteful grass—like the stuff Lash and Saul are in now. Only the marshes beyond. No nice trim fields like today . . . Any luck, Saul?' he called. 'No? Then let's get on. As it's such a bloody day and Mister Lash is having such a rotten time, we'll cut over to the thirteenth tee and start back home.'

'Aye, Master,' said Saul Bax.

Martin Lash, playing last off the thirteenth tee (and now facing back in the direction of the Club House), sliced his ball; with his horrible, hefty, heavy swing. The east wind gathered it and escorted it well over the Ancient Highway, which ran parallel (more or less) to the thirteenth fairway.

'Now watch out,' said the Brigadier. For the first time he accompanied Lash and Bax on their search, and beckoned me to follow with him.

'The watching woman spotted the running sailor,' said the Brigadier. 'A Dutch sailor, as it turned out. She gave a whis-tle towards the shore, but of course it didn't carry against the wind. She brandished a rusty pruning hook. But the Hollander disarmed her, thick, tough wench though she was. And then, because as well as being thick and tough she was juicy, had it up with her skirts and off with her maidenhood. And then stran-gled her to teach her obedience, and went on his way through the marshes. And was picked up by the King's Men in Sand-wich. He didn't, of course, speak a word of English, but they soon enough twigged what he'd been about, because on this occasion the wreckers made common cause with the Sandwich

Watch, wanting vengeance as they did for their look-out girl he'd raped and strangled.

'There's a stone to her memory just over there,' said the Brigadier, 'just to the east of the Ancient Highway.'

A handsome, grey stone, slightly and elegantly shouldered. From behind it a black mass of a screaming young woman rose up and with her talons rent the face of Martin Lash to tatters.

The woman vanished with a kind of squelch. Saul Bax laid Lash's clubs on the ground beside Lash's body, and eyed both of us as if making a calculation.

'Take him away to Mary, Saul,' said the Brigadier; 'his clubs as well. Mister Raven and I don't want to be buggered up with them the rest of the way home.'

'Aye Master,' said Saul Bax. Having concluded his survey of the load, he slung the bag of clubs over one shoulder and the body of Lash over the other, and trotted away on his bare feet over the fields (where the marshes had been once and in parts were still) towards the Cinque Port of Sandwich.

'A local boy, you see,' said the Brigadier; 'he knows the way.'

We approached the stone.

'You can't read it any longer. The letters are too worn,' said the Brigadier; 'but the Department of Works has kindly provided a crib.'

Near the stone a modest green notice (white-lettered) informed us that:

BY THIS STONE

IN AUGUST, 1782,

MARY BAX

AGED 23 YEARS AND NINE MONTHS

WAS MURDERED BY MARTIN LASH,

A FOREIGNER

WHO WAS EXECUTED FOR THE SAME

'No bloody nonsense in those days,' the Brigadier said.

'But surely,' I observed, 'this Martin Lash, with whom we've been playing, he can't be the man named here.'

'Oh no. A descendant, perhaps. Although the name is a happy coincidence,' said the Brigadier, 'it doesn't really matter to Mary Bax, in her vault near St Clement's ... where her brother is even now bringing her the food of her revenge. Since he's the man of the house, you see, he carries the game-bag. She just does the killing and finds her own way home.'

'Leaving with a squelch,' I said, remembering. 'Are you sure Lash was dead?'

'Doesn't really matter. Either way, they'll share him together in their vault. So long as it's a foreigner (as this notice you see expresses the case) it's all right with them. A foreigner like Lash—that one or this. Only if there's a long shortage of foreigners does Saul carry off an Englishman, so I make it my business to keep them well supplied with what they prefer. For the good name of the Club. We can't have Englishmen, let alone our own Members, vanishing into the earth.'

'How do they know ... when their kind of prey is available?'

'I tell 'em. There's a little hole through which you can talk into the vault by St Clement's. "Saul, Saul," I say, "Mary, oh Mary, you will have a visitor tomorrow. Come and collect him" (or "*her*"—they are in no way sexist) "at the usual time." '

'But won't someone miss him, sooner or later, someone back in Holland?'

'All busybodies will be told that Lash left this afternoon for Rye, where he has a booking at a reputable hotel. His hired car will be found parked on the road on the other side of Hythe. No Lash in it. No clubs. Total disappearance and mystery. I don't think—do you? that the police will look in the Bax family vault near St Clement's.'

'How did such a family come to have a vault?'

'They made a lot of money out of wrecking.'

'Why,' I enquired, 'did you invite me this morning?'

'You're an author. I want you to write an account of this business. Write an account, and send it to me—for publication around 2050 AD, long after you and I are safely dead. I'll see to that in my will. For the record, you understand.'

'I understand,' I said.

'And just add as a postscript,' said the lean Brigadier, with a thin-lipped giggle, 'that I hope to get a lot of Japs playing here before long. That shouldn't be difficult—they're swarming over half the courses in the country. A shower of Japs, on some business hospitality caper—that should keep Saul and Mary happy for a very long time,' the Brigadier said.

THE TRIC-TRAC MAN

For convenience' sake I shall call him Henry Whybrow. If you should wish to know his real name, you may probably be able to work it out by the time I am finished.

Once upon a time, one winter's afternoon (already nearly dark) in Piccadilly, I came across Henry, whom I had known for decades but not seen for several years; he was hanging about the entrance of what had once been the St James' Club, his magenta jowls heaving, his thick lips drooping, his hairy nostrils opening and closing like motor valves.

'What's happened to the Club?' he said.

'It's gone,' I said. 'Didn't you get the letter?'

'I've been abroad for some time.'

'Well, the lease packed in, or something of the sort, and all members were transferred to Brooks's . . . if they wanted to be.'

'What happened to the backgammon sets?' Henry asked.

'They went to Brooks's too. They were set up in a special room with a soothing Turneresque landscape. To keep the players sweet-tempered, I suppose.'

'Ah, I imagine that as a paid up member of the St James' I was transferred with everybody else?'

'I don't think it was automatic,' I said, 'but I am on my way there now, so you can come with me and see about it.'

Although I had never liked Henry very much, I'd had a soft spot for his wife Constance, who was long since dead and almost certainly dead of Henry; but I knew she would have wished, not being a vindictive woman, that Henry should be agreeably accommodated with a club now that he had returned (from wherever it was) to London. It was, then, largely out of affection for the memory of Constance that I was now assisting her bulbous relic.

'The Secretary is away,' I said, 'on a Sabbatical Year; but the Club Registrar Incumbent in his place will know the form.'

So through the dank London dusk we went, and down St James's Street, and up in the lift (belly to belly) in Brooks's, to see the Club Registrar Incumbent. To him Henry Whybrow explained who he was, his absence abroad (where? I wondered again) when the St James' Club had closed its doors, and his wish to apply, better late than never, to be listed as a Member of Brooks's. I then affirmed that Henry was indeed Henry, that he had been a prominent frequenter of the St James' before he went abroad, had always comported himself with as much propriety as could rationally be expected of him, and had punctually paid his dues.

'I see no difficulties here,' said the Club Registrar.

'Good,' said Henry, who had cheered up a bit in the last half-hour. 'Now then. I have only been a few hours in England, I have nowhere to stay and no luggage apart from this little bag (as Air Mongol has lost all the rest), and so I should very much like to put up in the Club for a few nights. I am sorry if it seems presumptuous, but needs must when the Devil, et cetera. No doubt you will be requiring my subscription: I shall have to ask you to wait until my assets have arrived from the Orient and are duly credited in Lloyd's bank across the street.'

'We allow a month's grace for payment of subscriptions,' the Registrar said.

'I shall settle with you long before that,' said Henry puffily. 'Let's see, what is the date? November the twenty-seventh? I shall be in a position to satisfy you at the beginning of next month. A matter of days.'

'That's all right then,' I said, as if for some reason my approval were needed.

'And can I have a room?' said Henry.

The Registrar Incumbent hesitated very slightly. Then, 'I can't see why not,' he said. 'I remember the instructions were that members of the St James' should be admitted without delay or formality. Of course you can have a room, Whybrow—if the porter on duty finds that one is available.'

That night we had dinner together, Henry and I. His appetite for food and drink, which had always been keen, was now ravenous. He contrived a six course menu for himself, accompanying it with half a bottle of champagne, a bottle of Chambolle Musigny, and about a pint of Chateau-d'Yquem. Between gulps and mastications he told me a little of what he'd been doing abroad.

'I've been all over the Far East,' he said. 'I decided to go when Constance died—get over the loss, you know. She left a tidy sum—I was quite surprised—so I thought: I'll go on a long tour—just the thing to help me get over poor old Constance.

'I didn't have to rough it, of course,' he went on over a quintuple measure of Marc-de-Provence, 'but every now and then I found myself in some pretty odd places. I was caught by the monsoon once in a garrison town in Mongolia. Complete outpost, hundreds of miles from anywhere. I spent the whole time playing chess and backgammon against the Commandant; funny chap, a combination of Greek, Russian and Amerindian.'

'How muddling.'

'Worse than that. His grandfather had been a Thracian but his father had been born in Georgia, and later exiled to the Arctic Circle, where he married an Eskimo squaw from Alaska. My man was now Colonel Commandant of his hyperborean garrison ... and, as I say, a very formidable wrangler at chess and backgammon. Taught me a lot about both games, especially tric-trac which was what he always called backgammon—that was the Greek coming out in him, I suppose. I used to think I was pretty good in the old days at the St James'—but nothing to what I was after a month of playing with him. I picked up every trick in the Asio-Oriental book and a good few extra. Helped me no end on later occasions. And that reminds me: let's see what's going on in that backgammon room you were telling me about.'

I played a couple of games with him myself, lost a few pounds, and passed him on to better players. His method wasn't at all the flamboyant affair which I might have expected from his account of his tuition. I had always understood that the finest exponents of backgammon were for ever on the aggressive, making deployments of hideous menace yet at the same time leaving long trains of 'blobs' which miraculously came together at precisely the moment of crisis. There was nothing of this about Henry's style of play. He didn't even take carefully calculated odds-on risks. He was as dull an opponent as it was possible for a man to be, always making the safe and dreary move, never leaving a lone piece unattended for one second longer than necessary. He never made a flashy move, never showed off. He just proceeded fast and smoothly round the board (but *how* one asked oneself, with such boring and moderate throws?) and was taking his men off before one had even begun to get one's strategy together.

'It's a knack,' he said when I congratulated him on his speedy passage. 'Just you spend a whole month of monsoon playing against a Greek-Russian-Eskimo, and you'd probably get it yourself.'

He had no spectacular triumphs. He was so swift round the board that there was little opportunity to double. 'Better that way,' he said, as we recorded his modest gain and my tolerable loss on the form provided and posted it in the appropriate box for the attention of the Registrar. 'Win a little here and there,' Henry said, 'and there's no hard feelings anywhere. I know how nasty people can be if you take them to the knacker's—I'll never do *that* again.' He did not expand on the theme but moved on to his new opponent, from whom, after five quick games, he had won just twenty pounds. No hard feelings. And then he took on someone else. . . .

At the end of the evening there were only Henry, myself and an elderly spectator left in the room. The elderly spectator, having quietly declined Henry's offer of a game, ordered drinks for the three of us and having thus bought himself a captive

audience, began to soliloquize in the relentless and urgent fashion of club *cognoscenti* throughout the kingdom.

'It is interesting to reflect,' he said to us, 'that gambling in the
Club went very much out of fashion for most of the nineteenth
century and the first half of the twentieth—was indeed resumed
only when you and your fellow-members from the St James'
came here to join us. But of course what passes for gaming nowadays is mere trifling if compared with what went on in the late
eighteenth century, when, for example, Mr Brooks first began
to manage the club that was later to bear his name.'

Henry's demeanour reminded me of a character called
Dead-Wide Dick, Captain of the School XI in the *Hotspur* (a
journal I much fancied in my infancy), who spent most of the
day apparently asleep but always woke up and went into amaz-
ing action as soon as a vital catch came his way or seventy runs
were needed in ten minutes.

'Go on,' Henry said urgently, having only a second before
appeared to be on the verge of coma; '*please* go on,' he said,
rather as though he expected the pandit to reveal the quickest
route to Solomon's Mines or Aladdin's Cave.

'Charles James Fox,' said our instructor vibrantly, as if
inspired by Henry's enthusiasm, 'Selwyn, Sheridan . . . Wilberforce . . .'

'*Wilberforce?*' I said.

'Oh yes. He was led astray every now and then. He even ran
a Faro Bank on one occasion. He had tremendous good luck—
and guilt commensurate with it. Then there was the drunk
duellist, FitzGerald, who would insist on playing here though
he wasn't a member—everyone was too scared of him to tell
him to leave. But perhaps,' said the elderly member, getting his
second wind, 'Mr Brooks the Manager was as odd a character
as any. He was such a toady that he would always advance large
sums, without any security, to any gentleman who was embarrassed for ready money at the tables, cash on the nail being the
rule, at least theoretically, at this period. The result was, of
course, that Mr Brooks was soon much embarrassed for money

himself. So he had a secret passage constructed by the Club servants; it started near the bottom of the present lift shaft and led to a small and secret niche which was excavated under the street. There Mr Brooks would hide when the duns came, well provided with a hamper and a piss pot.'

'Where did he empty it in the event of a long siege?' asked Henry, as if he ardently wished to know.

'Into the pipe that led to a conduit beneath. Mr Brooks became fond of his hide-out, which was just as well, since it was also his last resting place—or very nearly so. When he died, the duns came for his clothes and his cadaver, which in that age would have fetched a handsome price from chirurgeons engaged in anatomical research. So the servants bundled Mr B's body into his niche and battened down the hatches from outside until such time, a very long time, as the duns wearied of the hunt. By some sort of misunderstanding the wretched fellow was entirely forgotten. Only about ten years later, when a member, who had been (like you Whybrow) many years abroad, ordered a footman to "fetch Brooks your master and tell him to bring two hundred guineas with him," did people suddenly recall that Brooks was still in his niche under St James's Street. I'm happy to say he was given a regal funeral to make up.'

Henry rose. Although he had encouraged the soliloquist at the outset, it was plain that he had had enough now.

'I'm off to bed,' he said. 'I need to sleep long hours—some debilitating virus which I picked up in Mongolia.'

'Let me offer you luncheon tomorrow,' said the antiquary, who obviously still had hopes of Henry as an audience.

'I never eat lunch,' said Henry. 'Dinner, if you please . . .'

When I returned to London after a few days in the country, there was a note for me from the Registrar Incumbent asking me to call on him in his office.

'That man of yours, Whybrow,' he began.

'He isn't my man.'

'You introduced him. You should know that he is presenting problems.'

'Oh?'

'First of all, he won't leave his room till late in the afternoon. He locks the door, pins a note outside (on the new paintwork) saying "Do not Disturb until Four p.m. of the Clock," and simply cannot be roused no matter how hard anyone hammers.'

'Why should he be roused?'

'The servants want to make up his room.'

'Tell them to make it up after he's left it in the evening.'

'The kind of servants who make up the rooms have gone home long before that.'

'Rubbish,' I said. 'If somebody arrives to stay late and unexpected, the servants have to make up a room for him. It's always happening.'

'We have to call on the wrong sort of servants. It is inconvenient, and it is resented.'

'Then charge Whybrow extra.'

'I do,' said the Registrar. 'But here's another thing. He has a very odd way of paying his dues.'

'Is he in default?'

'Not exactly.'

'Either he is,' I said, 'or he isn't.'

'On the first of this month,' said the Registrar, 'about four days after you first brought him here, he came to this office around tea time, and he said: "By my reckoning I'm well over £270 ahead in backgammon." Which was true enough. I'd just had all the gaming slips in, as I do at the start of every month, in order to calculate the gains and losses of the previous month. Between his arrival on November 27th and the end of the month's accounting at midnight of November 30th, Henry Whybrow had won £276.80, which included £8 lost to him by you. Here's your statement; take it now and save me the trouble of putting it in an envelope.'

I took it, 'Then what?' I said.

'You pay it.'

'I meant, "Then what about Henry Whybrow?" '

'Whybrow said to me: "Please add up what I owe for my subscription up to December 31st, and for my room, and for all the food and drink I've had. Then deduct it from what I've won and keep the balance for my future credit. I hope to occupy that room indefinitely." '

' "You can't," I said. "Quite apart from the rule which states that no member can occupy a room for more than fourteen consecutive nights, the Christmas break is coming up in ten days' time. You will have to leave the Club from December 23rd to January 3rd. Everybody has to."

'He didn't like the sound of that,' the Registrar continued. ' "Christmas break?" he said. "Since when did the Club close for bloody Christmas?" Then he took a pull on himself. "Sorry," he said: "I mustn't get snappish. So be it. Book me in from January 3rd for as long as you can." "The porter on duty will do that," I said, "if it is possible." "Of course," he said, as mild as milk; "but you won't forget to take what I owe from my winnings—everything, laundry and all? And keep what's left as credit."

' "You can have what will be left now," I said, anxious to put an end to this eccentric arrangement; "I'll do my sums and write you a cheque." "Cash?" he said. "I haven't got enough cash," I told him. "Then just you hang on to the balance like a good chap," said Whybrow, "and debit all my dues as before." And with that he was off.'

'I don't see what you're grumbling about,' I said. 'You've been paid out fair and square, and he's leaving you some money to pay the next lot. I told you when I introduced him that he was never late in meeting his dues.'

'I just wish he'd pay with a cheque like anybody else.'

'Why?'

'It makes it easier for the books. And another thing, Raven. People are beginning to mutter about Whybrow's winning all the time at backgammon.'

'Does anybody say he cheats?'

'No.'

'Then they're just bad losers,' I said. 'I've watched him play. He doesn't play for a high stake, he doesn't get fierce with the doubling die, he plays an absolutely straight and pedestrian game with no tricks or evasions.'

'Exactly. He doesn't take risks and he concentrates a lot. He works the thing out. People say that isn't very sporting.'

'Simply because they're too idle or too stupid to work the thing out themselves. He finds plenty of chaps who want to play against him—or he wouldn't be winning so much.'

'They're all determined that *somebody* should beat him, that's why. They've become obsessed.'

'And whose fault is that?'

At dinner that evening I sat next to Henry at the Club Table. He enjoyed his food as greedily as ever, but was clearly in a huff.

'What shall I do at Christmas?' he said. 'No meals here, no backgammon, not even a bed.'

'Have you no friends and relations?'

'Not now Constance is dead. And if I had, what's the odds? We'd spend the whole time either simpering at each other or quarrelling about who should do the washing up.'

'You might persuade them to go racing. There's some first-rate meetings on Boxing Day.'

'I can't go racing any more.'

'Surely not warned off?'

'Of course not, or I shouldn't have been let in here.' He evidently disliked the topic but felt, now that it had been raised, that he must make his position clear. 'I find that ... these days ... I can't get up early enough.' He looked at me shiftily and gabbled on, 'What I mean is, for midwinter meetings, you have to set off at sparrow's fart.' He paused for a moment to assess the effect on me of this wholly unnecessary gloss, then said: 'Make myself clear?'

'I suppose so. It hardly matters.'

'No. Another annoyance,' he went on crossly, 'about the

Club's closing: the night before it closes there's a Dilettanti Dinner, and all the bedrooms have been booked weeks in advance, so I'm now told. As if it's not bad enough having the place shut on the 23rd, I shall now have to find somewhere else to sleep on the night of the 22nd.'

'You'll manage.'

'I dare say.' He grunted and went off to the backgammon room, full of wine of every colour but entirely steady as he went.

I next saw Henry on the night of December 22nd, rather late, nearly midnight, just as I was leaving the Club.

'Want to share a taxi?' I asked. 'If you're going anywhere near my flat?'

'No, thanks.'

He showed no signs of leaving himself.

'I thought you'd been kicked out of your room to make way for some Dilettante?'

'Oh yes. But I'm putting up very near here, only a step or two away.'

'Happy Christmas, then,' I said tactlessly.

Henry said nothing, but turned and walked towards the loo.

I hadn't meant to go to the Club at all on the 23rd. But when I called at Jackson's to pick up my Christmas order of caviare, the fellow said that it had been sent, in error, to Brooks's (where they often sent my stuff for me). The Club had closed at noon, but when I rang the bell, it was opened ... by a very discomposed Registrar Incumbent.

'I hoped it might be you,' he said. 'I saw an enormous parcel for you. It's just over there.'

'Thank God I could get in. Fresh Beluga goes off pretty quick.'

'Like corpses,' he said.

'Like what?'

'Come upstairs,' he said. 'The duty porter's just getting me some tea and crumpets.'

I looked at my watch. 'Three o'clock,' I said; 'I've got to get

down to Walmer in time for dinner. And I want to get that caviare in my refrigerator as soon as I can.'

'Come upstairs,' he insisted.

So up we went in the levitating sentry box.

'You know,' he said, after the porter had deposited his tea
tray, 'that I have always been slightly suspicious of your man,
Whybrow?'

'He isn't my man,' I repeated from an earlier discussion.

'No. Not any more. He's dead.'

'How? When? I saw him only last night.'

'He'd been dead for a long time before that,' the Registrar
Incumbent said, shaking so much that he dripped butter from
his crumpet on the knee of my new suit. 'I've been making
enquiries. The answers have just come in. He died in the East. A
considerable time ago. Some row over a game of chess or backgammon. The Russian police have made a special report at the
request of Scotland Yard. Some row with a Russian officer of
some kind.'

'But if Henry Whybrow is dead,' I said, 'the chap we have
had here has got to be an impostor. That would explain all
the business about not having any money in Lloyd's when he
joined, and not wanting to sign or receive cheques, and so on
and so forth. Just a con man scratching a living.'

'But,' said the Registrar, 'you were so *sure* it was Henry
Whybrow. And apparently nothing has happened since he's
been staying here to make you think otherwise.'

'I am a rational man,' I said. 'If Henry Whybrow is dead,
then I have made a silly mistake, and the man who has been
staying in this club has got to be an impostor and a crook. There
is no other explanation.'

'Oh yes, there is,' said Henry, coming through the door.
'Sorry to disturb you both. I thought, Registrar, that you
would have left by now for Christmas in the bosom of your
family; so I just popped up to check on my backgammon winnings for the last three weeks—I imagine you've called the slips
in as the place is closed till the New Year, and I shall be needing

the credit when the bills come in early in January. But as things have turned out, I am very sorry I came. It is not nice to hear an old friend call one an impostor or a crook.'

'What else can you be?'

'A walking stiff,' said Henry, and laughed rather a lot. 'A zombie, if you like, but not a crook. I agree, however, that I owe you both an explanation.'

'I told you, Simon, about my experience in that Russian Army outpost in Mongolia. Only I left a lot out. The upshot was that I began to beat my mentor at tric-trac, as he called it. What was worse, from his point of view, I also beat him at chess. People get very vain about their chess: King Cnut split the skull of someone forward enough to checkmate him—split his skull with a battle axe. That Russian, cooped up for years in that horrible place, cooped up cheek by jowl with me for weeks of monsoon, finally flipped his lid when I toppled his king, and then toppled me with his sabre. And while I was bleeding to death, he cursed me . . . with a ghastly Thracian curse he'd learned from his father, who, being Georgian for good measure, was doubly versed in magic. The curse was that I should rise from my grave at dark on the day of my burial and wander the earth—the old Wandering Jew syndrome, you see—wander the earth for ever. And to make matters really foul, I was to endure the torment of never being able to lose at chess or backgammon. You see the point? Theologians say that the most cruel punishment in Hell is being *unable to fail, for ever and ever, amen*; always and for ever having instant sexual success, or writing a masterpiece automatically every time you put pen to paper, or, in my case, being unable to lose at chess . . . or tric-trac.'

'At least the curse provides you with an income,' said the Registrar sourly.

'That's just the point,' said Henry. 'I've paid my way by tric-trac, under the most hideous and often insanitary circumstances, all the way from Inner Mongolia to the West End of London. Now that I'm here, I am hoping to settle down and play in a civilized and gentlemanly fashion, and otherwise to enjoy a little peace and quiet. And then what happens? You close the Club on me. It's a dreadful thing to ask a fellow to change his whole way of life—or should I say death?—at my age, if only for a few days over Christmas. You've no idea of the problems. To start with, I can only get about when it's dark. And then for as long as the light lasts the next day I have to lie in a sort of trance, like Dracula—though I swear to you I'm not a vampire. But I have a huge appetite for food, because if one is dead one needs immense resources to keep one quick—if you take my meaning. Very often I can't get at food for days, the limitations on my movements being so severe, and so when I can I simply stuff myself like Vitellius. I've been doing that for the last few days to keep me going over Christmas until the Club reopens.'

'I see,' I said; 'and why do you drink so much?'

'For the extra calories. If you're dead, you see, you get no pleasure from it, and you can never get drunk (that's part of the curse), but the calories are an essential item of your heavy diet.'

'That's all very well,' quavered the Registrar, 'but where are you going to spend Christmas? You should have left the Club by noon.'

'Don't be so inhospitable,' said Henry. 'I thought of the bed-rooms, but they're all locked and there'll be a relay of porters on duty sniffing round the place, so in the end I decided I'd spend Christmas in Mr Brooks's niche. You remember,' Henry said to me, 'when that old fellow told us about that in the backgammon room on my first night? At dinner the next day I wormed a lot more useful details out of him—the probable approach to the lair, and so forth. As soon as I knew for certain I'd have to leave my room, I reconnoitred the passage and tidied up the cell, and I've just been spending a tolerably comfortable sixteen hours there.'

There was a long silence. Then the Registrar, who had for a time become much calmer, so soothing and sensible had been Henry's mode of discourse, started to shake again.

'But what on earth am I to do with you?' he said. 'Stick a stake through your heart when you're in one of your comas?'

'I told you,' said Henry sternly: 'I am not a vampire. I should just be walking about with a stake through my body, thus creating a scandal. Whereas, if you leave me as I am, nobody need ever know anything derogatory about me.'

'You're not thinking of staying on in the Club?' said the Registrar Incumbent.

'How else am I to li–, er, exist? The Club is the ideal solution. Somewhere to sleep all day—Mr Brooks's niche when I can't have a proper room; excellent food and drink—not that I can actually enjoy it, but the kind of robust country house cuisine you have here is superbly nourishing for one in my condition; and then that agreeable backgammon room in which to make my li–, that is, my means of subsistence. You will have noticed, surely, that I am not being greedy for a guaranteed winner? I know I can't lose, but I only win as much as is strictly necessary for one in my sad situation.'

Henry paused and looked at both of us.

'You wouldn't have the heart,' he said, 'to turn me out?'

And of course, though neither of us really likes Henry, we haven't had the heart to turn him out.

After all, he does no harm. Some chaps like him much more than I do. He has some entertaining tales about the East, and particularly about Mongolia. He makes no demands. The Registrar has found him a flowered chamber pot to furnish the niche when he's in residence, and every now and then I smuggle down a hamper from Jackson's. No; Henry Whybrow is no trouble to anybody. But I thought you might be amused to learn that one of your fellow-members is—well, let's face it, a Ghost, albeit a very mundane one. He is not, as I said at the beginning, actually called Henry Whybrow. I expect you'll guess his real name: a chap who's never seen by day; is always in the Club by night; eats and drinks like Gargantua; has heavy magenta jowls and a proboscis that functions like some bivalvular device; and spends hour after hour in the backgammon room. If you rumble him, don't betray the poor fellow. How would you like to be under an eternal curse which never allowed you to get pissed and took all the excitement out of backgammon?

FAIR ROSAMUND

'Two to one the field,' proclaimed Syd Shroud of Folkestone (BPA).

'What price Fair Rosamund?' Nicholas inquired.

'Ten to one to you, sonny,' leered Syd.

'I'll go and tell Daddy.' Nicholas said to me: 'He could be interested in Fair Rosamund at ten to one. Where shall you be watching the race?'

'I'm going to miss this race,' I said. 'I'm going to have a look at the Castle.'

'Why?'

'My dear Nicholas, we've all been coming to Folkestone races since you were a baby in a basket. Can you ever remember a time when I didn't visit the Castle?'

'But why?' grizzled Nicholas, scratching the crutch of his corduroys. 'Just a rotten old ruin by the railway with a lot of grotty caravans around it.'

'Three fine 14th-century towers.' I said. 'And a good stretch of the east wall. Up against the wall there's a very handsome farmhouse—certainly not a ruin. Early eighteenth century but as good as new. Why not come too? You could join me after the race.'

'No thank *you* very much.' Nicholas said. 'Mummy took me a couple of years back and I simply hated it. There's a beastly moat full of brambles and fleas and rubbish from the caravans. And that farmhouse of yours—it's falling apart.'

'All it needs is a little attention, and it'd be as sound ... as sound as it was when Fair Rosamund lived there.'

'Fair Rosamund? Not the horse?' said Nicholas, and giggled.

'Not a horse. A lady whom Henry the Second loved.'

Nicholas frowned.

'Henry the Second,' he said sanctimoniously correcting an adult, 'was a long time before the eighteenth century and a pretty good time before the fourteenth. So the lady he loved couldn't have lived in the farmhouse or even in the Castle.'

'There was another castle—or at any rate a house—before they built the 14th century one on top of it. A lot of the stones are the same. So one can say, in a sense, that Fair Rosamund lived within the same walls. They've even named one of the towers after her—though I agree with you that she couldn't exactly have lived in it.'

'The tower of Fair Rosamund,' said Nicholas, his imagination caught. 'I don't think she'd have liked those caravans much.'

'She might have been glad of them. She had a very boring life here, you know. There was no race course then, there was nothing—nothing for miles and miles. She could have done with a little distraction.'

'But surely ... being the King's *mistress*,' said Nicholas boldly, 'that must have made up?'

'It's not usually much fun, being a king's mistress.'

'What happened to her?'

'The King took her to Woodstock.'

'I see. Now I must go and tell Daddy there's a good price for the horse. I'm going back to it anyhow. I s'pose it was named after her ... like the tower?'

'Very probably.'

'So if the horse won ... I ought to come and say "thank you" to the lady?'

'It would be courteous certainly.'

'All right. So I might be meeting you there after all. If you see me coming you'll know it's good news.'

My godson lolloped off to find his father. I walked away from the stand, crossed a little meadow in which some scattered official cars were parked, and approached the moat. Full of brambles and rubbish, as Nicholas had said. On the other side of it was the east wall and, looming at its northern end, The Tower of Fair Rosamund; not the corner tower but the square one a little way to the west of it. Or so they said. Some people, of course, denied the story altogether. One of the more celebrated guide books was emphatic: 'There is no reason whatever to suppose that Fair Rosamund ever set foot in this part of Kent.' Well, perhaps there wasn't. But I liked to believe it, and I was going to go on believing it. And besides, I had set my godson off believing it. I would not wish him to be disillusioned.

'Fair Rosamund,' I said aloud: 'let his horse win. Then I shall know that you have lived here.'

The little trees rustled all along the wall and the wasps flickered in the garbage.

I went round behind to examine the caravans, which were on the lawn of the former farmhouse. Would they have annoyed her? It was hard to tell. One knew so little about her except her name. The name conjured up a rather ample lady, blond and bland, easy and good-humoured, glad to swap a simple jest with the caravan folk. Or did it? Could it not also suggest a glittering snow white fairy, a sprite of the woodland, some creature out of Ariosto who would appear to benighted travellers in the forest, perhaps kindly . . . and perhaps malign?

I returned to the meadow by the moat. A roar from the stand announced the end of the race. Quarter of an hour passed, but Nicholas did not come. Perhaps he's collecting his winnings first, I thought. But the minutes ticked on and still he did not come. At last I made myself realise that Fair Rosamund had not won and that Nicholas had therefore, and quite equitably, not come to thank her. Does this also mean, I thought to myself, that the lady never lived here? Oh, don't be so ridiculous, I thought: whether she did or she didn't, why should she bother to answer my prayer for a race-horse or to enlighten me about her place of residence eight centuries ago, even if she had the power to do so?

As I walked out towards the paddock, where Nicholas and his father should now be inspecting the runners for the next race, I passed the results board. Third Race, it read: 1. Fair Rosamund: S.P. 12 to 1: Tote win 204p. Place 57p. 2. Jill-a-my-Nory . . . Fair

Rosamund it was, then, after all. Since Nicholas, I knew, would have backed it on the Tote he would have won nearly 20 to 1 for his wager. And yet he had not come to thank the lady as he had promised. Not like my godson, who could be often silly and sometimes greedy, but was of a chivalrous disposition.

Nicholas's father was standing by the rail of the paddock, fidgeting.

'Have you seen Nicholas?' he said.

'Not since before the last race. He left me to find you.'

'He did. He tipped me Fair Rosamund, but like a fool I decided against it.'

'Did he back it himself?'

'Oh yes, I went to the Tote with him and we watched the race together. Then he said something about meeting you by the Castle and saying "thank you" to the lady.'

'I waited some time there. No sign of him.'

'But he went immediately after the race. He was so anxious to tell you the news. He'd had a whole pound on that horse. What did he mean, about saying "thank you" to the lady?'

I explained.

'Well, I suppose he can take care of himself. Must have missed you, that's all.'

'He couldn't have missed me.'

'Then he changed his mind and went somewhere else. But where on earth is he? The next race is in five minutes. Are you *sure* he couldn't have missed you?'

'Not if he went the usual way—across the meadow to the moat. I suppose . . . that he could have gone the long way round, through the wood near the railway. It depends on which way he went with Josceline. The only other time he ever went was with her. "Mummy took me," he said. Two years ago.'

'Josceline would have taken him through the woods. She likes woods, Josceline does.'

Together we walked round the paddock, past a group of huts and along the path into the wood. Nicholas was coming the other way.

'Have you thanked the lady?' I called as he lolloped towards us, his corduroys sagging slightly at the waist.

He didn't answer or wave, but came on to meet us. Or rather, not to meet us. His face, while still smooth, and lightly freckled, still flecked with silver down on the cheeks below the temples, had shrunk and twisted into that of an old man. Black eyes looked blankly beyond us. He walked straight on. When we realised that he would not stop, we parted to let him pass between us.

'Nicholas?'

He did not pause in his walk.

Fair Rosamund had heard my prayer and answered my question. Now she was exacting her price. Because I had doubted? Or because she had been so bored and desperate in her tower of the wilderness during the long days before she went to Woodstock?

THE GUIDE

A corbel grinned beneath the eaves; beneath the corbel two knights in low relief had at each other with stubby lances.

' "A curiously placed sculpture," ' Gwendolin read out from the guide-book, ' "to commemorate the death in a tournament of one of the Royal Princes of England." '

'Why,' said Gilbert, 'should a Prince of England be commemorated on the outer wall of a church in France?'

'Because we owned all this bit. The castle at Suscinio, just a few miles away, was an important English garrison.'

'The castle was later,' said a low, pleasant voice behind them.

They turned to look at a slender man whose handsome but slightly wizened face was framed in a grey woollen scarf which he had tied with a knot over his head, like the cloth round a steak-and-kidney pudding.

'The castle at Suscinio,' said the man, 'wasn't built until the thirteenth century. That carving'—he pointed up at the two knights and their frumpish mounts (more like sheep than horses, Gwendolin thought)—'that carving,' he said, 'was made quite early in the twelfth. But you are right about the English ruling this territory. Most of the time, anyway. Before the castle was built the English had a camp here at Saint Gildas, and sometimes the English knights and nobles were billeted in the Abbey served by this Church.'

He moved round the apse by which they were all standing, walked along the eastern exterior of the north transept, and then turned to beckon Gilbert and Gwendolin.

'Please come here,' he said

They looked at each other, shrugged, and went to join him. When they came up with him, he pointed obliquely, past the nave of the Church, to a wide gateway in a high wall. Through the gateway were flowers and grass. A nun looked out. She had a soft, pretty face and wore her dress down to only a few inches below the knee, as nuns do nowadays. She smiled at them all from the distance and called out merrily in French to the man in the scarf, who waved back.

'The Cloister,' the man said, 'the Cloister of the Abbey of Saint Gildas-de-Rhys. Very different now from what it was when that carving was made. No flowers then. Mud, dung and a granite well. No nuns either. Monks. Bloody awful brutes who couldn't even speak French, only the local Breton. The only one who wasn't a brute was the one who made that carving.' He pointed back towards the apse. 'He'd been trained as a mason, and one of the English noblemen who were billeted in the Abbey somehow found this out. So he told the good brother to make a carving in memory of the English Prince who'd recently been unhorsed and had his neck broken in a jousting match at Winchester. The monk wasn't keen on Englishmen and made a pretty poor job of it, as you'll have remarked for yourselves.'

'What marvellous English you speak,' Gwendolin said.

'I was with General de Gaulle in England from forty-one to forty-four,' the man replied. 'Then I was rather nastily wounded in the Normandy landings and got shipped back to an English hospital. I was there nearly a year. Plenty of time to learn.'

'But that was a whole generation ago,' said Gilbert.

'I have a long memory, *m'sieur*. And I like the English. Unlike this monk I've been telling you about. In fact the fellow botched that carving far worse than now appears. But he was ordered to tidy it up and make it at least halfway decent by the Abbot. Abbot Abelard.'

'*The* Abelard?'

'Oh yes. Peter Abelard was Abbot of Saint Gildas-de-Rhys, for a time at least. After he'd been castrated by Heloise's relations for bringing disgrace on her family, he went into the Monastery of Saint Denis. He became a monk there and was allowed to go on lecturing and writing. But of course the

other monks were jealous. They said that because he had been
... still was ... a celebrated man of letters he was being given
privileges. They pointed out that when all was said and done
he was now a eunuch, "an abomination to the Lord ... stinking
and unclean." The authorities said that this wasn't altogether
his fault, but all the same they decided to get him out of the
way ... which suited him well enough, for he was sick to his
back teeth of all the eunuch jokes and imitations that had been
going on, and he longed to escape from the spiteful pettiness of
Saint Denis and live in a clean and remote country, where he
might meditate in peace on God's truths. So at his suggestion
the authorities sent him back to his native Brittany—he was
a Breton by birth, you know, son of an *écuyer* who held land
near Nantes—and made him Abbot of Saint Gildas here. The
idea was that since he was a pretty formidable sort of fellow he
might be able to civilise and discipline the monks.'

'Although he was a eunuch?' Gwendolin said.

'They thought that country bumpkins would be so over-
whelmed by having a famous man of learning as their Abbot
that they'd toe the line out of sheer reverence. But not a bit of
it. The monks here despised him for his scholarship as much as
they did for his caponhood. Anyway, they couldn't speak his
language and he couldn't speak theirs—'

'... But you said he was a Breton ...'

'... Not the sort of Breton that speaks the sort of Breton
that they spoke round here in 1126. That was the year he came.
The year in which the young English Prince was killed at Winchester and Lord Otho of Lewes commanded the monk-mason
to sculpt the memorial on the outer wall of the apse. Abelard
arrived to find the memorial botched and Lord Otho in a fury.
Since he wanted peace to contemplate the Nature of Things
and not red-faced English barons raising Cain all round the
place, Abelard told the monk to mend his work ... which the
monk, albeit reluctantly, proceeded to do. He, at least, could
understand Abelard and respect him. But when the rest of them
heard about it, moronic Bretons that they were, they flew into a

kind of nationalist frenzy—no, not nationalist, *separatist*. Who was this la-di-da gelding from Paris to order a decent Breton monk to obey an English Lord and honour an English Prince . . . a Prince of Norman descent, of course, which finally topped it all off. If there was one race which you poor, fey, clownish Celts really hated, it was the practical and acquisitive Normans.'

'Abelard should have taken the Bretons' side,' said Gwendolin. 'Those monks *were* his people.'

'Not really. He was born far away from here on the Nantais border, the son of a nobleman . . . however petty. He was in any case a man of the world . . . such as it then was . . . and of great intelligence. Above all, as I say, he despised squabbling and wanted peace.'

'Did he get it?' asked Gilbert.

'No. His monks were addicted to drink, thievery and copulation, in ascending order of preference. He was rash enough to rebuke them. They might have forgiven, in time, his intervention in favour of Lord Otho, but when he tried to interfere with their established way of life, they rebelled totally.'

'Serve him right,' said Gwendolin. 'Sour grapes, if you ask me. He and Heloise, back in Paris, had carried on like a pair of monkeys; but now that he couldn't do it any more, here he was trying to spoil everyone else's pleasure.'

'Yes,' agreed Gilbert. 'All those pious hymns, when the man was just a common lecher. "O Quanta, Qualia,"' he quoted, '"Sunt illa Sabbata." "How many and mighty are the Sabbaths." *He* wasn't in a fit state to tell Saturday night from Sunday morning. They never stopped . . . until her uncle Fulbert found them at it. Why, he owns up to it himself in his autobiography, whatever it was called . . .'

'" . . . *Historia Calamitatum*," said the man in the scarf: "*The Story of my Misfortunes* . . ."'

' . . . Well, he owns up there. He was doing it so much, he says, that his work was going to pot. I read it in an extract in the *Reader's Digest*. It sounded exactly like one's Housemaster warning one against masturbation.'

The man in the scarf nodded.

'But there is another way of looking at it all,' he said:

> ' "*Ou est la tres sage Helois*
> *Pour qui fut chastre et puis moyne*
> *Pierre Esbaillart a Saint-Denis?*
> *Pour son amour eut cest essoyne.*"

> ' "Where is the learned Heloise
> For whom Peter Abelard was shorn
> And mewed up into a monk's chemise,
> Paying quit for his love with loss of his horn?"

'He didn't, so to speak, get away with anything. He didn't even find the peace he'd hoped for at this Abbey. A little compassion is called for, I think.'

'It wasn't roses all the way for Heloise either,' Gwendolin said. 'Because of him they sent her off to a gungy convent.'

'At least the other nuns didn't try to poison her. That's what the monks here did to Abelard.'

'Only because he stuck his nose in where it wasn't wanted. Anyway, our Master Pierre was much too sly to be caught that way, I bet.'

'He survived, and excommunicated all the brothers . . .'

'. . . How pompous . . .'

'. . . Whereupon they hired robbers to murder him. And when that failed, they threatened him, in his own parlour, with naked daggers. Finally he escaped through a secret passage.'

'Trust him,' said Gwendolin crossly, 'the original slippery Dick.'

'He certainly had astonishing luck,' said Gilbert. 'I really can't see why he was always being so sorry for himself . . . or why we should be expected to be so sorry for him. It was hard cheese having his apparatus chopped, I grant you that, but he knew, as well as any man living, what the penalty was for that sort of behaviour in that sort of society. A little more self-

control would have been in order. After all, the chap was a don
... and at quite a decent college, by French standards.'

'Anyhow,' said Gwendolin, 'they made it up to him in the
end. Didn't they put him and Heloise in the same coffin?'

'So it is always said.'

The man in the grey scarf looked away towards the Abbey.
The soft, pretty nun again appeared in the gateway. Again she
called to the man, this time not merrily.

'Why is she crying?' Gwendolin said.

The man loosened the front of his trousers. Gwendolin saw
something white and woolly that resembled a baby's diaper
violently flecked with crimson streaks.

THE SPIRIT OF CRICKET TO COME

I belong to a cricket club which goes on a summer tour of three weeks: Kent, Somerset and Shropshire. In the old days (fifteen years ago) the tour used to last four weeks, the final one being spent at a preparatory school owned by one of our number in Cumberland. We used the school as a country house; and in its grounds, at the bottom of a sloping lawn that descended terrace by terrace from the four regency bays at its rear, we played visiting sides from all over the north-west of the kingdom. Sometimes we all stayed as long as ten or fourteen days, arranging extra fixtures *ad hoc* after the conclusion of the official card, unwilling to part, dreading our return south.

This was the magic time of our club which, though still alive and indeed much increasing in youth and number, has never been quite the same (at least, not for me) since our host and his school dwindled and died, and the weeks in Cumberland ceased. I remember clearly the day that marked their passing; the day of the match against Penrith. While our side was batting (second) and the afternoon became evening, I was aware that a sturdy figure with a barrel chest and longish hair, dressed in what looked like a pyjama suit with a pattern of rust-coloured, horizontal hoops, was sitting on the roller, almost, but not quite behind the bowler's arm at the Pavilion End. Nobody is entitled to sit on a club roller unless he is a member. This man was a stranger. The captain and I went to warn him (gently) off.

'Good evening,' said the captain. 'Can we do anything for you? Is there anybody you want?'

'No,' said the stranger. 'Just watching. No objection, I hope?'

'None. Indeed not. But there are seats—deck chairs and so on—for visitors. This roller—well . . .'

'Of course,' said the stranger politely. He rose and smiled pleasantly, altogether transforming his hitherto rebarbative appearance, though I was still far from keen on his rust-hooped pyjama suit. 'I must apologise, gentlemen. I had forgotten how to behave in company on occasions like this. I must introduce myself: I am the Spirit of Cricket Future, of Cricket to Come.'

'Oh?' the captain and I said.

'You know,' said the man, 'like in *A Christmas Carol*. There's the Spirit of Christmas Past, and of Christmas Present, and of Christmas Future or Christmas to Come. I correspond, as far as cricket goes, to the last of these . . . though I try not to be so dismal.'

'You're not dismal or dreary at all,' said our captain, 'and we are honoured to see you here.'

'Civil words and thank you,' said the Spirit of Cricket to Come, 'but I'm afraid I bring disagreeable tidings. Mind you not everyone would find them disagreeable, in fact many would yell with joy at hearing them, but I do not think the people on this ground will welcome my message.'

'That must depend,' said our captain, 'on what it is.'

'This is doomed for a start,' the visitor said, waving round the ground with one hand and then up towards the school with the other. 'You must understand that all this will be done with before very long.'

'Yes, I had guessed that things were going wrong,' the captain said. 'There was trouble about ordering the beer this year. We keep two barrels down here for players and visitors, you see, and two on the top terrace. Well, for the first time since we've been coming here, we found no credit with the locals, for beer or for anything else. "You're from the school, ain't you? Cash," they all said. I have already made a mental note that this year will probably be our last here.'

'I wasn't speaking only of what is happening here,' said the visitor. 'As it happens, of course, you're right; within a few months this school will be bankrupt and the friend who lets you use it will be dead. But that's by the way. I meant . . . *this kind of thing. That's* what has got to end. Cricket weeks on the private grounds of private houses. It really won't do, you know.'

'Why not?' said our captain, with his calm and habitual courtesy. 'We're doing nobody any harm.'

'You're doing something that most other people cannot.'

'Anyone can play cricket that wishes,' I said.

'Not in circumstances like these,' said the Spirit of Cricket Future. 'You're being exclusive. You're keeping other people out.'

'We play all sorts of sides from all over the country,' said our captain, 'from village sides and even hamlet sides to Carlisle itself. We welcome spectators—as you yourself have just been welcomed—and we invite them to sit on our grass or our chairs and to drink, in moderation, of our beer. What's exclusive about that?'

'You haven't quite understood me,' said the Spirit of Cricket Future, rather sorrowfully. 'Of course I know that you're friendly to all comers, and free with your refreshments and the rest of it. What's exclusive about you lot is your attitude of mind. Almost anybody can play cricket, as you say, and a lot of people could get up cricket weeks pretty much like you do here, if only they'd take the trouble. The point is that most of them just don't want to. They like coming here to play you, once in a way, but they wouldn't dream of laying on anything like this for themselves. Or certainly not in your style.'

'Why not?'

'It's too peaceful,' said the Spirit of Cricket to Come, 'it's too decent. Those terraces are too elegant, that building is too distinguished, too beautiful. It might all be happening 150 years ago. The whole thing is a deliberate denial of this day and age. No car can get down to the ground. No one stays up at the school in case the telephone rings.'

'Why should anyone?' I said.

'There might be an emergency. Someone in one of your families or someone belonging to one of your opponents—*someone* might be ill or even dead. But none of you gives a damn about that. None of you gives a God-damn if the telephone goes crook and stays crook for weeks on end. So long as you can confirm your fixtures from the local call box, that's all you care about. And then the cricket itself is much too sporting. If one of your side is given out, however unfairly, out he goes without a murmur; and if a visiting player, in the same situation, does his nut or makes a hullabaloo, you all just look at him with quiet deprecation and probably let him stay at the wicket in order to avoid any further row. He has committed a grave error in taste but he is your guest and must be deferred to. He is perhaps of the working class and so he must be humoured.

'There are no quarrels on your side,' continued the visitor, 'about who shall open the batting or bowling or whose turn it is to be captain. You have one captain who always has been and ever more shall be so. None of you would dream of faking an injury to gain sympathy or to excuse incompetence. None of you would beg off fielding because you were needed by the wife to help with the kids. Come to think of it, there are no wives or kids—not of *your* club anyway—to nag and squeal on the boundary. There are no grievances here—or, once again, not as far as your members are concerned—no complaints, no thieving of other people's kit or money, no voices raised, no ice-cream van with a jolly jingle and no notice saying TOILET— you all just piddle in the bushes and, as for the women, you simply don't care if they burst.'

'Ladies can go up to the school,' said the captain; 'they only have to ask.'

'I told you. The school's too distinguished. It makes them uneasy to go somewhere like that for a pump.'

'For all that you say, a lot of sides like to come and play against us.'

'Yes. For once in a way, as I said. And of course they enjoy the beer. But they wouldn't want all this as a regular thing for themselves. It's just not right, it's not with it, it's a huge irrelevance.'

'All right. But it's *our* irrelevance,' the captain said. 'We like to do it. No one else need join in unless he wants to. Why then, for God's sake tell me, why has it all got to disappear?'

'Because,' said the Spirit of Cricket Future, 'it's going to be the same with cricket as with anything and everything else. It's not a question of "If I can't, you mustn't," it's a question of "If I don't want to, you mustn't" . . . just to make sure you see, that no one's having something which someone else isn't having.'

'But what does that matter . . . if the someone else that isn't having it has no wish to have it?'

'Perhaps he's missing out on something just because he's too dim to appreciate it. Unfair. Best to forbid it altogether. The long and the short of it is that most people can't bear to think of you and your friends having your polite and peaceful games without being bothered by anything in your stylish park, with your pretty terraces, with your Georgian or Regency house— in which you will later have dinner at 8.30 after a nice bath, and *not* high tea right after the match still wearing your nasty, sweaty cricket duds. This isn't just envy, either. *Most people simply do not want these things for themselves* but they'll do their utmost to see that you don't have them either.'

'But *why*?' our captain insisted.

'Just in case they *are* really missing out without knowing it. And anyway, how dare you want what they don't? How dare you have and enjoy it when they wouldn't touch it? And that,' said the visitor, waving and beginning to walk round the boundary towards the River End, 'that is the message of Cricket Future. Or rather,' he said, turning, and briefly halting, 'it would have been and it certainly should have been, but for this—all cricketers are and will continue to be such a silly, sentimental, inefficient, drunk and easy-going sort of crowd (for all I can do to them) that they won't, in the end, have the heart to interfere with you. This place, as we've been saying, is going down the black hole pretty soon,' he said; 'but there will always be somewhere else and you and those like you will find it.'